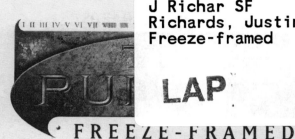

I II III IV V VI VII VIII IX

PU

· FREEZE-FRAMED ·

ALSO BY JUSTIN RICHARDS

In the *Invisible Detective* series:

The Paranormal Puppet Show

Shadow Beast

Ghost Soldiers

Killing Time

The Faces of Evil

Web of Anubis

Stage Fright

Legion of the Dead

TIME RUNNERS

· FREEZE-FRAMED ·

JUSTIN RICHARDS

SIMON AND SCHUSTER

SIMON AND SCHUSTER

First published in Great Britain by Simon and Schuster UK Ltd, 2007
A CBS COMPANY

1 3 5 7 9 10 8 6 4 2

Simon & Schuster UK Ltd
Africa House
64–78 Kingsway
London WC2B 6AH

A CIP catalogue record for this book is
available from the British Library

ISBN 10: 1-416-92642-9
ISBN 13: 9781416926429

Typeset by Rowland Phototypesetting Ltd,
Bury St Edmunds, Suffolk
Printed and bound in Great Britain by
Cox & Wyman Ltd, Reading Berks

For Nancy — another Special Agent!

· CHAPTER ONE ·

Let me tell you about the day my life ended. I remember it as if it was yesterday, which maybe it was. Or perhaps it will be tomorrow. I lose track. After all, it was a long time ago.

Rewind: I need to start a day or two before that. When I first saw Anna, and when Midnight came looking for me.

It was after the end-of-school rush. I always waited for most of the other kids to leave. I'd go to the library or my form base and get my homework done. Easier than trying to do it at home with my little sister, Ellie, making a racket and Mum and Dad on my case. Easier to say, 'Yeah, I've done it.' And it meant I didn't have

1

to leave school with everyone else – the walkers and the bus children, upper school, teachers, the lot. I'd rather be on my own.

There were still a few other kids about and I recognised some of them. But it was a huge school. There were more children in my year than there were in the whole of my old school. I was the only one who went up from my primary school to Oakridge that year, but we'd moved into the middle of town and it was just down the road, so I could walk. New home, new school.

'You'll soon settle in,' Mum kept saying. 'You'll soon make friends and join clubs. You'll soon know loads of people.'

'It's OK,' I told her. 'I'm fine.' Though of course I hated it. Funny, that – you never appreciate things till they're taken away from you.

So there I am (or was, or will be), just coming out of the main block and starting along the drive. And that girl with the crooked, nervous smile is Anna – waiting. Certain it will do no good to speak to me, but knowing she has to try.

I thought she was just another schoolkid. She looked about that age, a year or two above me. Fourteen perhaps, maybe fifteen. But she wasn't wearing a purple school jumper or dark blazer. Someone's sister? I didn't really think about it. I didn't really notice what she *was* wearing – the pale blouse and loose skirt both held tight at the waist by a big belt.

I suppose it looked a bit out of place. Especially her watch. A flat black disc with a thin black strap. I noticed that, poking out the end of her sleeve. It looked kind of neat and cool, and I guess it didn't really seem to fit with the rest of her image. But when you're twelve and you hate your school and wish your parents would leave you in peace and someone else would adopt your kid sister, you really don't think too much about fashion.

'Jamie!'

I actually turned right round. Must have looked daft, staring in the wrong direction.

'It's me,' she said. 'Anna. Only . . .' She sighed

and pouted and shook her head. 'This is a waste of time.'

'Sorry,' I said. 'Do I know you?' Some older sister of a friend of Ellie's, I thought.

'You will. Unless you listen to me.'

Which sounded odd, and I probably laughed. I looked at my watch – I remember clearly that it was four minutes past four. The second hand was just grazing the number one. I barely glanced at it, though, just making the point that I wasn't going to hang around.

'I don't have much time,' I said. And *she* laughed, though I had no idea why she thought it was funny. Not then ... And it annoyed me, so I said, 'Yes. I've got homework to do. Need to check stuff out on the internet.'

She frowned, the smile gone. 'Internet?'

'My computer. Well, my dad's.'

'You have a computer?' She seemed astonished. 'At home?'

'I really have to go.' But I didn't move, just watched her.

She glanced over her shoulder, towards the science block, and suddenly her face was set and

4

hard, like she was trying to stay calm. Like she'd just been asked about homework she hadn't done and was going to bluff it out. Her eyes were cat-green, and her nose turned up ever so slightly at the end, finishing with a tiny flat bit. Her fair hair looked like it had been scaffolded into place with enough spray to withstand a hurricane. She was quite pretty really, I suppose.

'You're in danger,' she said, voice level and low. I must have looked like I really was about to leg it, because she added, 'Not from me, you twerp.'

I'd never been called a twerp before and I blinked in surprise. 'What?'

'Danger,' she repeated. 'Midnight is after you. I didn't think you were that important, but *he* does. Look, we don't have long.' She glanced over her shoulder again, and I saw someone looking back, from the shadows beside the science block. Just a shape, a silhouette. But it unsettled me.

'What are you on about?' I demanded.

'You said you had no time. Do you . . .' She frowned, trying to decide what to say and how to say it. 'Have you any idea what *time* actually

5

is or how it works? Where it comes from and where it goes? How you can travel through it as if you're on a journey? How it behaves and . . .' She paused, swallowed. 'And what lives inside it?'

'I've really got to go,' I told her.

I started to walk away, but she grabbed the strap of my rucksack and pulled me back. She was slight and slim, but a bit taller than me and stronger than she looked. She almost pulled me over.

'Lay off!' I dragged myself free. 'Go and hassle someone else.'

'No, wait.' She sounded afraid more than anything, and that frightened me. 'Listen, please – you must, or you'll be lost.'

I shook my head, turned and hurried away.

'Be kind to Ellie!' she shouted. 'You'll need her.'

I probably flinched at that. But I didn't stop. She was still calling after me, but I didn't listen any more, didn't look back. Didn't look at anything or anyone – the world could have been frozen around me as I marched head down out of school, away from the crazy girl.

When I got to the gate, I risked a look back. She was still watching me, but she turned away as I looked, and walked slowly towards the science block and whoever was there. I looked at my watch, not because I was wondering how long I'd been talking to her, but because I always checked the time when I got to the gate.

Four minutes past four. The second hand was just grazing the number three. I didn't think about that, I didn't really take it in. I looked back towards the science block, in time to see the girl talking with someone in the shadows. They were partly hidden behind a laurel tree. But I could see it was a boy. I only saw his silhouette, but he looked slightly shorter than her, younger . . . In a strange way, he reminded me of myself. The two of them, talking – that must have been how she and I had looked just a minute ago.

The boy glanced up and saw me. I still couldn't make him out. But I knew he'd seen me because he turned and walked quickly away, behind the building. The girl stared at me for a moment longer, then she followed.

*

7

That evening, Midnight came.

Ellie was sitting at the breakfast bar, swinging her short legs and drinking milk through a curly straw. Except the beaker was pretty much empty and she was still sucking – enjoying the throaty, gurgling sound it made.

'Don't do that, Ellie,' Mum said, without looking up. 'You had a good day?' She meant this for me.

'Yeah,' I told her.

Mum stopped chopping whatever vegetable it was we were going to have to eat tonight and looked at me. She obviously expected more, but I just wanted to forget about it.

'Science was good,' I said, hoping this would be enough. It wasn't, so I said, 'And we had history too.' Dead boring, I didn't add. Mum likes history. Used to like. Will like. Whichever it is.

I went to pack my rucksack for the next day. Mum was shouting something after me, or maybe at Ellie. I wasn't listening. I turned my music up loud and read an old comic book. I'd read it before, loads of times, so I knew all the stories.

But that just makes them funnier – when you know what's going to happen. Well, it's only drawings. Not like real life.

We didn't wait for Dad for tea because he was working late. I managed to keep Ellie out of my room, though she shouted from the other side of the door about playing some game or finding some toy. Or something. I had my 'Girl-Free Zone' card hung on the door handle, so I didn't answer. Anyway, I was reading.

The guest vegetable was broccoli and I didn't eat it. Mum glared, and I knew she'd give what I left to Dad with his dinner later. And he'd leave it too. Ellie talked non-stop, but she didn't say anything interesting. I tuned out.

'You're very quiet,' Mum said, when we'd finished and I was helping to clear the table.

'No,' I told her, 'Ellie's very noisy. I couldn't get a word in.'

'Well, she's gone now. What were you going to say?'

I shrugged. 'Dunno. Can't remember. Nothing much. When's Dad coming home?'

There were some letters on the hall table.

They had stamps, so I went out to the post box. Ellie was practising her recorder so no way was I staying indoors. You can't hear yourself shout when she's blasting away on that. Tuneless, random notes – endless, boring. Nothing like real music.

It was getting dark already and the street lights had come on, so the world was tinged with an orange glow. It was good to be outside and on my own. I was whistling, I realised, as I stuffed the letters into the box. One was too big and I had to fold it over and force it in. Something of Mum's. I pushed my hand right inside the slot to be sure the big envelope dropped down properly and didn't get stuck and left behind when the postman emptied the box. The top of the opening caught my knuckles – cold and hard.

When I turned back, there she was again – on the other side of the street. Anna. There was a bloke with her. But it couldn't be who she'd been with at school, because he was taller than her, a grown-up wearing an old-fashioned trilby hat. I could see them both clearly as they stood under the light on the pavement outside Mrs

Heggety's. She's complained to the council about it and they fitted a bit of metal on the back so it doesn't shine into her bedroom. The metal sort of forces the light down on to the pavement in an orange puddle, and that's where Anna and the man were standing.

I thought they were staring at me. But they were looking past me, I realised. I turned to see what they were looking at, but there was nothing there – just the post box standing by the hedge. And when I turned back, they'd gone.

I gasped out loud – saw my breath in the cold evening. Where could they have gone? How? One moment they were there and the next . . . Had I imagined them – an old-fashioned-looking girl and a bloke in a trenchcoat and a hat? Gone. I turned back to the post box. Not sure why. Maybe I thought when I looked again they'd have reappeared.

The church clock was starting to strike the hour. Must be seven o'clock, I thought. I started to count.

One . . .

There was a man beside the post box.

Two . . .

He was wearing a dark cape and a top hat and holding a silver-topped cane.

Three . . .

He stepped out from the shadows and the orange light made his face glow. He was smiling, and tapped the brim of his hat with the top of his cane by way of greeting. His face was angular – almost sharp, so his features caught the light and made patterns of shadows across his face like rippling water or smoke.

'Hello,' I said, startled. I had been half listening for the next chime of the clock.

'Good evening, young man,' he replied. His voice was rich and deep and dark, with a hint of amusement in every word, and I realised how quiet everything suddenly was. 'My name is Midnight,' he said, stepping towards me.

Midnight – I vaguely recalled the name from what Anna had said. But I didn't make the connection, not then.

'You seem perplexed,' the man continued. 'Can I help?'

'I was wondering where they went,' I told him.

'Did you see them? A girl and a man.' I pointed. 'Over there, by the light.'

'And now they have gone,' he agreed. 'I wonder who they were.'

'The girl's called Anna,' I told him. 'I met her this afternoon, after school. I'm sorry, I'm Jamie.'

He nodded, as if he already knew. 'Jamie,' he repeated. 'Jamie Grant, who lives in the end house and who, sadly, doesn't like history.'

I gaped. 'How do you know that?'

The man shrugged, but he was still smiling. 'Didn't you tell me?' He did not wait for me to answer. 'You say you've met this girl Anna before?'

'After school,' I said, still confused. 'I don't know her, she was just nattering on about ...' I wasn't sure what she had been nattering on about. 'About time and stuff.'

'Time?'

I turned away, suddenly embarrassed at being asked. 'She said something about knowing how to travel in time.'

'Did she?' We were walking now. I had set off down the road, back towards the close, and he was walking with me. His cane tapped on the pavement with each step. Otherwise it was quiet, so very quiet. Just the tap of his cane and the sound of his voice as he said, 'The problem, surely, is not so much the travel as proving that you were ever away.' He raised the cane and tapped at the empty air in front of us. 'How would you do that, do you suppose?'

'What do you mean?'

He sounded like he was making an effort to keep his patience. 'If you travelled into the past,' he said stiffly, 'how would you prove to anyone else that you'd been there? It isn't like going on holiday. You can't just send a postcard. A photo from the past. A snapshot, to show you there while it happens around you.'

'I s'pose not.'

'So, you'd have to find some other way to – what shall we say? – to put them in the picture.'

'Yes.'

We had reached the turning into the close. The man – Midnight – stopped and again tapped the brim of his hat with the end of his cane. This time it was a farewell rather than a greeting. It was a strangely timeless gesture – like his clothes and his manner. I could imagine *him* fitting into the past quite easily.

'Till we meet again,' he said quietly. 'As we surely will.'

I watched him walking away down the street, barely aware that the clock was still striking. Or had it started striking again?

Four . . .

He seemed to fade into the shadows, melting into the night as he went. For a moment I thought I saw something running along beside him – a dog or perhaps a fox. Low and dark, with a staccato scuttling motion. Claws tapping like his cane on the ground.

Five . . .

I waited for Midnight to reach the glow from the next street lamp. Then I would see what was with him, keeping to the shadows and the darkness. But he never got there. He seemed to have faded away into the gathering night. I turned and started into the close.

Six . . .

Heading back towards home. The end house.

Seven.

While in the distance, the church clock finished striking the hour.

CHAPTER TWO

🕐 12TH OCTOBER

Next morning it started. My alarm went off as usual and I got up and got dressed and went down for breakfast. We eat at the breakfast bar in the kitchen, sitting perched on stools that are too high and too narrow, and Ellie fidgets a lot. Mum puts out the bowls of cereal and cutlery – spoon, and a knife in case we want toast afterwards. She was sitting there already with Ellie. By the time I came down, Dad had already left for work. Ellie was still in her pyjamas. She had milk down her chin.

I went to sit in my usual place. But there was no bowl. No cutlery. Nothing. Like Mum hadn't bothered. Or just didn't think. And she was staring at me like I was a total stranger.

Then Ellie said, 'Hello, Jamie. Mum didn't get you a bowl. I don't know why. Perhaps she forgot.'

And Mum blinked and wiped her face with her hand. She looked tired. 'Sorry,' she said. 'Yes, I forgot. You sit down, I'll get it.'

I smiled at Ellie. Well, Anna had told me to be kind to her and at least *she* hadn't forgotten I lived here. Ellie stuck her tongue out at me and giggled. Who'd be five again? I thought, and looked away.

Mum was by the fridge, frowning. She'd poured milk over the corn flakes and now she was looking down at them, confused. 'Do you want sugar on these?' she asked.

I laughed. 'No, thanks.' I never have sugar on them. Every morning – corn flakes. Every morning – no sugar on them.

'Of course,' she muttered, setting the bowl on the breakfast bar. 'There you are, James.'

She never calls me James.

*

18

It got worse at school.

Mr Makepeace did the register, as usual. He does it every morning in the same tone of voice. All surnames, in alphabetical order. It's like a ritual, a prayer, that we all intone under our breath. Only this morning it was different.

'. . . Dodgeson . . . Evans . . . Feynman . . . Finch . . . Finklestone . . . Genassi . . . Ibbotson . . . Jeffries . . .'

What? It doesn't go like that. A few people exchanged glances. A few turned to look at me – ready to say 'Yes' and then not being asked.

'What about Grant, sir?' Charlie Jeffries asked as his name was called.

'Who?'

'Me,' I said. I stood up. 'Grant. It goes Finklestone, Genassi, Grant. Then Ibbotson and Jeffries.'

Mr Makepeace stared at me as if I was mad. Peering over those little round glasses that he thinks make him look cool but actually make him look sad and old.

'Grant,' he repeated after a while.

I nodded. 'Jamie Grant.'

I could see him writing carefully in the register – more than just a tick. The very end of his tongue poked out between his teeth as he did it. Then he looked up and smiled reassuringly at me.

'Welcome to Oakridge, Grant,' he said. 'You'll soon settle in.'

It wasn't the way that Charlie and some of the others laughed that upset me. It was the way that some of them didn't. Like they really thought I *was* there for the first time that morning.

In Geography I actually knew the answer for once when Miss Farrel asked a question. I stuck my hand up, sure she would pick me. But she didn't.

Then later, in Mr Clarke's French class, when I put my hand up I was the only one.

'No one?' Mr Clarke said. 'No one at all?'

I was straining, reaching for the ceiling, almost standing up. 'Sir!'

He turned and wrote the answer on the board. Like I was invisible or something.

The boys I sat with at lunch didn't talk to me

at all. I said stuff, they ignored it. I gave up and ate my food. In afternoon classes it was like I wasn't there at all.

In History we got new textbooks – about how we lived a hundred years ago or more. It looked pretty boring. Mike Ibbotson was handing them out. He went right past me, missed me out.

'Hey!'

He turned and looked at me. Then he turned away again, shaking his head. I glanced round, wondering if there was someone behind me, egging him on, playing tricks. But all I saw was a glimpse of myself, reflected in the small window in the door. Looking back at me. I looked so sad. So I stood up and grabbed a book off the top of the pile Mike Ibbotson was holding.

'Thanks,' I told him, sitting down again. 'Thanks for nothing.'

He just went on handing out the books. I stared at the cover in disbelief – why was he ignoring me? Why was *everyone* ignoring me? They paid as much attention to what I did and said as the children in the sepia-toned photo on the book cover.

There were maybe a dozen of them. Boys and girls in old-fashioned clothes, grouped in front of a stone wall and staring seriously at the camera. One of the boys was wearing a jacket that was much too small and his tie was undone. Next to him, a short girl with dark hair was looking nervous. She was wearing a pinafore dress and clutching a doll made of cloth.

After a day like that, it was almost a relief to see Crazy Anna after school, watching me from the other side of the street. The pelican was already going, so I crossed over quick, before the lights changed again, and ran up to her – suddenly afraid she'd disappear before I got there.

'Looking for me?'

'Why would I be looking for you?'

I shrugged. 'Thought you might have some more crazy talk for me. Like yesterday.'

She was shaking her head, starting to walk away. I kept pace with her, as she said: 'I didn't talk to you yesterday.'

'Don't be daft. After school, on the drive. Then in the evening I saw you by the post box, only you . . .' I couldn't tell her she'd vanished – how stupid is that? 'You went away.'

'Midnight came,' she said quietly. There was a sadness in her voice and she avoided catching my eye, looking away. 'I didn't realise until *then* that you were important.'

'Oh, cheers.'

She looked at me now, those emerald-green eyes holding me in a fierce stare. 'So I wouldn't have spoken to you before that, would I?'

'Well, you did,' I protested. 'You spouted some rubbish about time being like a journey or something and told me to be kind to Ellie.'

She quickened her pace. 'I have no idea what you're talking about. I don't know anyone called Ellie.'

'She's my sister. She's five and she's a pain.' I hurried to keep up. 'And if you didn't talk to me, how come I know your name, then, *Anna*?'

She stopped so suddenly I was several paces past her before I realised. I turned back and saw that her face was twisted into something between pain, confusion and worry. 'Why would I risk *that*?'

23

It unsettled me. I didn't want to ask what she meant. 'So where's your friend?' I said. 'Where's that guy in the trilby hat?'

Her expression didn't get any better and her eyes were moist with tears. 'He's gone,' she said.

'Gone?'

'Midnight took him . . .' she started. Then she stopped and shook her head. 'You wouldn't understand.'

'Thanks.' I carried on walking, and this time she struggled to keep up with me. 'All day people treat me like I'm not here, and now I meet someone who'll actually speak to me and you're just talking rubbish.'

'Are you lost?' she asked quietly – almost like she wasn't asking me at all, but talking to herself.

'No, I live here. Or just over there, anyway.'

'You may be in danger.'

'Yeah, you said that yesterday.'

'Midnight wants you. You must be very important, though you don't know it.'

I wasn't sure about that. 'Midnight? If you mean the bloke with the top hat, the cape and the stick, he seemed nice enough.'

She shook her head. 'Keep away from him. He's trouble. Trouble like you wouldn't believe.'

I stopped and turned to face her. 'Yeah well, so you say. But he made more sense than you. He talked about time too, and what he said I actually understood.'

'What *did* he say?'

There was an urgency in her voice and she took hold of my coat – like she was going to pull me towards her and make sure I answered. It was weird, because I thought I could feel something else pulling as well. Thought I could see, just out of the corner of my eye, a tiny, claw-like hand pulling at my rucksack. Shadows, that's all.

I dragged myself away, though she was still holding my coat, and my rucksack shifted precariously when I moved – again, like someone had pulled at *that*. Just the weight shifting.

'I dunno,' I told her. 'Can't remember. But he said something about how it would be difficult to prove you could travel in time because you can't just write a postcard home and say "Hey look at me, I'm here having tea with Henry VIII." He said you'd have to find another way to put someone in the picture. To prove you can do it.'

'Proof,' she murmured thoughtfully. But I didn't ask her what she was thinking. I should have done, of course.

Instead, I pulled away again, and my rucksack slipped off my shoulder. It fell to the ground and the clasp came undone. It does that when it's too full. Books scattered across the pavement as if someone had deliberately pulled them out and tossed them around. I muttered angrily and bent down to retrieve them.

Anna helped me stuff them back into the rucksack. She picked up the new history book, which had landed at her feet, and looked at the cover. 'Put you in the picture,' she murmured. I think that was what she said, anyway. Then she thrust the book back at me.

'I'll talk to you later,' she said.

'Yeah. See you,' I replied, not looking. I was too busy forcing my rucksack closed and getting the clasp to shut. I straightened up, heaved it on to my shoulder again and set off towards home.

There was no sign of Anna.

*

26

I had to ring the bell three times before Ellie opened the door to let me in.

'Thanks,' I muttered.

'I don't think Mum heard you,' she said. 'She's in the kitchen.'

The bell rang right outside the kitchen door. I rang it again before taking my shoes off. No response.

'See,' Ellie said. And then she leaned round the door and rang it herself.

In a moment Mum appeared from the kitchen, drying her hands on a tea towel. She stopped when she saw me and Ellie, and sighed.

'I thought there was someone at the door,' she said.

'There was,' I told her as Ellie shut the door behind us.

'Just stop messing about, Ellie. You know I'm busy.'

Ellie looked at me and shrugged before scampering off upstairs.

'Yeah, thanks,' I said. 'It was really good. Great lessons, fantastic lunch. People keep ignoring me, but who cares?'

Mum had already turned and gone back into the kitchen. I wondered if I should follow her. But she was obviously in a mood, so I took my rucksack upstairs to my room.

Ellie was sitting on the floor of her room with picture books spread out round her. She wasn't really reading them – just pointing at each picture in turn and humming tunelessly. She looked up as I paused in the doorway.

'Thanks for letting me in,' I said.

She nodded, and went back to her books. 'Your friend's here,' she said. 'I let her in, too. Mum's busy.'

My friend? I wasn't expecting anyone. Mum kept asking me if I wanted to ask anyone home for tea, and I kept telling her no. But maybe she'd talked to one of the mums from my old school. Maybe it was Leo.

Except Ellie had said 'her'.

I realised who it was as I opened my bedroom door, just before I dumped my rucksack and saw her lying on the bed watching me. So it wasn't a surprise, not really.

'Hello, Jamie,' Anna said.

'Ellie told me you were here,' I said. I didn't know what else to say really.

She pulled herself up so she was leaning against the pillow and the headboard. 'Yes, Ellie can still see you. She's still young enough, untainted by time. But she'll grow out of it. One day even *she* won't know who you are.'

'What do you mean?' I laughed, but it was a nervous sort of laugh. I felt suddenly empty inside. 'What do you mean she can still see me? I'm here, aren't I?'

'Are you?' She sounded sad.

'Don't be daft.'

'You don't keep much stuff in your room,' she said.

My room was a tip. Mum was always on at me to tidy it. She said she'd forgotten what colour the carpet was. Dad said I had too much stuff, but I didn't want to get rid of any of it. You never know when you might want a toy or a book or . . .

My desk was clear.

The shelves were empty.

The walls were bare.

Even the bed, now I looked at it, wasn't made.

It was like the bed in the spare room, with the coverless duvet folded up and caseless pillows against the headboard.

'What's going on?' I breathed, looking round in complete disbelief. Finally I looked at Anna. She still looked sad, and I could tell she knew what was happening. 'What's going on?!'

'You'd better sit down,' she said. She shuffled across so I could sit next to her on the bed.

'Well? Why did they clear out all my stuff?'

'They didn't. You don't have any stuff.' She was looking at me closely, waiting to see how I would react. I tried not to react at all, to keep my expression completely neutral. To give nothing away. I didn't know what to think – *how* to react. But whatever I thought, I didn't want her to know.

'As far as your mum and dad know,' Anna was saying, 'as far as anyone knows except Ellie, there is no such person as Jamie Grant.'

I simply sat there, staring at the bare walls of the empty room. I could hear what she was saying, but it just sort of sank in without leaving a mark. Like my brain was quicksand.

'For a while, you'll be able to convince people you're still here. You talk to them and they'll notice you. But otherwise they won't. And it'll get harder. Soon they won't react if you just speak. Oh, they'll have to take notice of you if you stand in front of them and shout, or if you tap them on the shoulder. But you are fading. And it's worst, most advanced, here at home. This must be close to where it happened, or is happening, or will happen.'

She put her hand on my shoulder. I glanced at it, then looked away.

'I told you that time is like a journey, didn't I?' she said. 'That's what you said I told you. Well, like any journey, you don't have to go in a straight line, from minute to minute. You might decide to take a short-cut. You might change your mind about where you're going and head off somewhere else entirely.' She paused and looked at me sadly through moist eyes. 'Or you might get lost. You might wander off the path and never find your way back.'

'But I'm not lost,' I said levelly.

'You are now. Because something has happened

to take you off the normal path through time. It doesn't matter when it happened – or most likely it hasn't happened at all yet, but it will.'

'But I'm still here,' I protested. I thumped hard at the mattress. 'See?!'

'No,' she said quietly. 'You've been taken outside. And because of the way time works, that means you were never here at all. If you can make your parents see you, and maybe you can, they'll just see you as some kid who's bothering them. They won't know who you are, who you were. They never had a son called Jamie.' She sighed and waved her arm, gesturing at the empty room. 'Not ever.'

'It's a trick. A game. You're lying!' Even though I didn't believe that, even though I knew somewhere deep down that what she was telling me was true, I was angry and shouting.

Anna waited until I'd calmed down, lapsing into silence again. 'It's not a game, Jamie,' she said quietly.

I just stared. Then I turned to go, to ask Mum who I was and maybe hug her tight while she told me not to be silly. But I hesitated, only for a second, and in that second I felt Anna's hand on my arm.

'It's no trick.' I turned slowly round, and she looked down at the bed, avoiding looking at me. 'It's no use talking to your mum. Even if she remembers you now, she won't in a few minutes. You are one of the lost. It's hard for you, I know.'

'How can you know?' I demanded. I grabbed her shoulder, turning her so she had to look at me. There were tears in her eyes. 'How can you possibly know? My whole world is falling away from under me, how can you have any idea what that's like? To lose your family and friends and . . .' I struggled to think of a word big enough. There wasn't one. 'And everything. How dare you tell me you know what it's like?'

She didn't look away. One of the tears spilled out and ran gently down her cheek.

'I was lost in 1955,' she said quietly. 'It was a warm summer's day and I was fourteen. I'm *still* fourteen. And that was years ago.'

I didn't say anything. But I reached up and wiped the tear from her cheek with the side of my thumb.

We just sat there in silence for a while. Who knows for how long. Then I said, 'This is crazy. Stupid. Daft. There's got to be some reason. I mean, like Mum's ill or something. Ellie knows who I am. It's Mum's problem, not mine.'

Anna sighed. She pulled herself along to the edge of the bed and stood up. 'I knew you wouldn't believe me,' she said quietly. 'I knew you'd never understand, without proof.'

The clock in the hall was striking.

'It'll be teatime soon,' I said.

She just smiled, sadly. 'You'll find out,' she said. 'You'll learn, like I did. You'll have to.'

Anna kicked my rucksack gently with her toe – just enough to topple it on to its side. 'Look at the book,' she said. 'The history book you got today. Just take a look. And I'll see you later.'

I stayed on the bed after she'd gone, staring at the blank wall where my posters used to be. There was no sign of them. No dry smudges or marks from the sticky stuff or tape. Nothing. Like they were never there.

Somewhere in the distance, Mum was shouting. 'Ellie, it's time for tea. Go and wash your hands.'

And that was it. I knew – just knew – she wasn't going to call me.

I got off the bed, walking through a haze like I was someone else. I opened my rucksack and tipped everything out. The history book landed face down. I picked it up and flicked through the pages. It seemed normal enough – what was Anna on about?

With a grunt of annoyance, I tossed the book on to the bed. It landed cover side up. And at once I saw what she meant. The photo. I didn't touch the book – didn't dare. I sank to my knees beside the bed and stared at the picture on the cover. The picture of the children. There it was. Proof. A postcard from another time.

The sepia-toned children stared back at me just as before, serious as ever. Except for one. It must be a different photo, I thought. But no – there was the boy who was too big for his jacket, tie undone. Next to him there should have been a small nervous girl clutching a cloth doll.

I could see the doll, lying on the ground, a small hand reaching down for it. But I couldn't see whose hand it was. Because next to the boy with the small jacket, standing where the girl with the doll should have been, was a different girl. She was taller, smiling falsely for the camera, wearing a pale blouse and a loose skirt with a wide belt pulled tight round her waist. There she was, in a picture, which the caption inside the book cover said was taken in 1905, and printed on the cover of a textbook goodness knows when – looking just as she had five minutes ago and grinning, I was sure, *at me*. It was Anna.

I don't know how long I just knelt there, staring at the cover of that book, staring back at Anna. It was dark by the time I went downstairs. I felt numb and empty, and I wasn't at all surprised that Mum and Ellie had gone ahead and had their tea without me.

With Ellie's help I convinced Mum she remembered who I was. But I could tell that I was slipping away – it was harder than at breakfast. I had to actually tug her sleeve or tap her on the shoulder for her to even see I was there at all. And from what Anna had said, it would get harder yet. There had to be something I could do – there must be some proof that I was who I said I was.

My great-aunt got funny when she was really old. She used to forget who you were if you just went out of the room for a bit. It was like that with Mum. She made me a sandwich, then forgot who I was and why she was making it even before she'd finished. I didn't want to sit and watch telly with her and Ellie, because I just knew that when she looked round and saw me sitting there she'd be startled and say, 'Who are you? Where did you come from?'

But there was nowhere else I could go. Even if I went round to Leo's or something and begged to stay in their spare room, they wouldn't know who I was. They'd laugh, or slam the door in my face, or call the police.

And what would the police do? Even if they could see me, they'd assume I was lying about who I was – I mean, if my own mum and dad wouldn't own up to me . . .

The only thing I could think of to convince them, to try to turn the tide my way, was photos. My parents don't take many photos – not like Leo's mum, who's always got her camera with her. But there's a drawer of holiday snaps and stuff like that in the living room. I got out a wallet of photos from some get-them-quick developer shop or other. 'Only an Hour' it said boldly on the front in faded scarlet. Yeah, right, I thought.

They were pictures of last year when we went down to Devon and got stuck in the traffic for hours and Dad knew a short cut that wasn't. Surely this would do it? Surely if I showed the pictures to Mum she'd remember who I was? I mean, you don't take complete strangers on holiday, do you?

Only I wasn't there. Like Anna said, I never went to Devon. Mum and Dad and Ellie smiled back at me, out of focus and braving the weather. Empty landscapes where I should have been. But wasn't.

'That was our holiday last year,' Mum said kindly. Ellie had gone up to bed, and I had sat next to Mum on the sofa – so she couldn't ignore me. We were looking at the photos together. 'It was so cold and windy.'

'I know. I was there.'

'Were you?' She nodded. For a moment, I thought she was beginning to remember, almost

39

dared to hope. Then she said, 'With your own family? I'm sorry, I've forgotten your name again.'

'Jamie,' I said through gritted teeth. 'Jamie Grant. I'm your son. I was there. You must remember.'

I grabbed her arm and she didn't pull away. She just looked at me like I was weird and sad.

'We went on the beach that first morning,' I said quickly. 'It was pouring with rain and Ellie was desperate to see the sea. And Dad and I dug a huge trench in the sand and the water came up it – much quicker than up the rest of the beach.'

Her face cleared. 'That's right, I remember.'

I breathed a long sigh of relief. I could have cried.

'Yes,' she went on. 'A deep trench, in the sand. For the water. Ellie must have been exhausted.'

'Ellie?' I was shuffling through, looking for a photo – the picture of me and Dad by our finished trench, leaning on our spades looking proud.

'All that digging she and her father did.'

There it was. The trench was a dark shadow in

the sand and the image was smudged by the rain that was still pouring down. But Dad looked proud, brandishing his plastic spade. Beside the trench. Alone.

'I really think it's time you were getting home,' mum said. 'Thanks for bringing ...' She broke off, puzzled and confused. 'For telling me ...' She gave a little laugh, as she stopped trying to recall why I was there. 'Well, thanks,' she said.

And suddenly I wasn't there any more. She was looking at me, but focusing behind me – looking right through me.

I grabbed some blankets from the airing cupboard. At least I didn't need to worry about Mum or Dad finding me in the middle of the night.

Ellie was in bed, looking at a book. I said goodnight. I wasn't sure she'd even heard.

'Why has Mum taken everything out of your room?' Ellie asked as I turned to go. She didn't look up.

'You shouldn't be going in my room,' I snapped back. 'You didn't ask, did you?'

'Sorry. I just wondered.'

I sighed, and went and sat at the end of the bed, watching her engrossed in her book. Eventually she looked up.

'Mum doesn't know who I am any more,' I said quietly.

'No,' she agreed. I was surprised how sad she looked. 'I keep telling her, but she forgets.'

'Thanks for trying.'

'Are you going away?' she asked, tight-lipped, like she was frightened even to ask.

I bit my lip and nodded. 'I suppose.' I hadn't thought about it, but I couldn't really stay.

Ellie was frowning. She looked like she was trying to make up her mind about something important. 'You can stay in my room,' she said at last. 'If you want.' She wriggled across the bed. 'I can budge up.'

'Thanks.' I stood up. 'But it's nearly time for you to go to sleep.'

She looked relieved. 'Will you be here in the morning?'

I paused in the doorway. 'I don't know,' I told her. 'I really don't know.'

She nodded thoughtfully. 'OK.' And went back to her book. I don't think she was ignoring me or being unkind. It was just like her mind had taken in as much as it could and now she needed to go back to something else. Something easier. An escape.

I couldn't escape. And I couldn't sleep either. My own mind was in a whirl – round and round and round, but thinking nothing. Just trying to work it all out, to replay Anna's words, to cope with what was happening to me.

I heard Mum saying goodnight to Ellie and putting her light out.

I heard Dad come in, late. When he comes in late and we're already in bed and asleep he always comes into our rooms to say goodnight anyway. So many times I've pretended to be asleep and he's stood there, listening to hear the sound of my breath. Then he pats me gently on the shoulder and whispers, 'Goodnight, Jamie. Till tomorrow, then.' And he tiptoes out again. He doesn't know I'm awake, doesn't know I'm listening, but he says it anyway. Perhaps he thinks I can somehow hear him in my dreams and will sleep more easily knowing he is home and that he cares.

Or perhaps he knows I'm not really asleep.

I heard him come home. I heard him go into Ellie's room across the landing.

I knew he wouldn't come into my room.

'Goodnight, Dad,' I whispered. 'Till . . .' But I couldn't say any more because my voice wasn't working. It had got stuck somewhere so that all that came out was a sob.

🕐 13TH OCTOBER

I helped myself to breakfast. Ellie said good morning to me and Mum looked at her oddly. Mum didn't say anything, just tutted and pushed the fridge door shut while I was trying to get the milk.

I didn't have the right books for school – just what was in my rucksack from the day before, the books that had spilled out on the pavement. Including the book with Anna on the cover. She was still there, grinning at me. And I think it was seeing her smiling face that got me through the walk to school. I had to find her – no one else could help me, even if I could make them listen.

The first thing I did was go to the History department. I wanted to check that it wasn't some clever trick, though really I knew already. But I found a shelf where there were several copies of the history book. All with the same cover. Half a dozen sepia-toned Annas smiling back at me from the desk as I spread them out.

The other children ignored me as they headed off for lessons at the start of the day. A day with no lessons – no need to go to school. If someone had told me about this just a week before, I'd have leaped for joy and whooped and shouted and punched the air.

Instead, I sat on the bottom step outside the main reception. I picked bits of gravel off the concrete and made a small pile in the palm of my hand. Then I took the gravel piece by piece and tossed it back out into the driveway.

The first lesson ended. Then the second. At morning break, kids streamed out past me. I got a knee in the back at one point, but no apology. Like I wasn't there.

'Are you all right?' a voice asked from behind me.

'Hello, Anna,' I said, without looking. 'What do *you* think?'

She sat down next to me and I held out my hand. She selected a few small stones from my collection and threw them one by one after mine. The kids out on the playground ignored us.

'I think we need to talk,' she said.

'Yeah. Is this why you came here in the first place – to warn me?'

She shook her head. 'We didn't know about you.'

'So why is this happening?'

She shrugged and threw another stone. 'Somehow you're caught up in it. In the time break.'

'And what's that?'

'It's something that's wrong with time. Something that disturbs its flow – like a breakwater stops the waves from coming in, or a windbreak changes the way the air flows. It's a problem, caused by something happening that shouldn't.'

'Something this Midnight bloke has done?'

'Possibly. Or it might just have happened. Or it could be that someone who doesn't understand how things work is trying to change time.'

'Change time?'

She had run out of stones and dusted her hands together. 'Look, if you could go back in time, and you accidentally killed your own father or mother before you were born, then you would never exist.'

'That'd be daft,' I told her. 'I wouldn't do that.'

'You *couldn't* do that,' she said. 'Because it would mess things up so badly. Do you exist or not? And if not, how could you do it?' She stopped and shrugged again, as if it was all clear.

'I see.' I didn't really, not the detail, not clearly. But I could sort of understand the shape of what she was saying. 'And this time break has been caused by something like that – something impossible happening. What does it look like?' I wondered. 'Where is it?'

'You'll know it if you see it.'

'So when'll it happen?'

'Maybe it already has. Whatever has gone wrong might have happened today, or yesterday or a hundred years ago or more. If it's something small, then it could take a long time till the effects are so severe that a time break appears. Remember the journey through time?'

I nodded. 'Someone's taken a wrong turning, is that what you mean?'

'Something like that. Time might only be off course by a little bit to start with, when the event that caused this actually happened. But little by little it veers further and further off the proper track.'

'And this time break appears when it gets too far away from where it should be – when things are really wrong.'

'When we fall off the cliff that should have been miles away,' she said quietly. 'When time itself falls off the cliff and gets torn to bits.'

'And what does falling off a time cliff look like?'

She shrugged. 'Depends. All we know is that it will appear, soon. Remember where you met me yesterday, outside the school?'

That didn't seem important compared with time falling apart. But I nodded.

'That's where the break in time will be,' she said. 'Or near enough. That's why I was there. Not to see you.' She looked away, as if embarrassed by what she'd said.

'Thanks,' I muttered. But as I did, I felt suddenly, physically sick. Right in the base of the stomach. I could feel myself become light-headed and hot and pale.

Anna was looking at me again. 'You feel it too, don't you?' She looked pale as well – but frightened rather than ill. 'He's coming.'

'What? Who?'

She leaped to her feet and I struggled up after her. I was feeling a bit better now, but still weak and heady.

Anna was looking round, anxious and urgent. She picked up a big pebble, weighed it in her hand, tossed it lightly in the air several times.

'We don't have long,' she said quietly. She tossed the stone away.

It stopped. In mid-air, it suddenly stopped. Frozen. Halfway to the ground.

Beyond the stone, a boy was running for a ball. Caught in mid-step. The ball stuck in the air in front of him. A girl was poised over a skipping rope – her hair still going up as she started to come down. Not moving.

A shadow passed over us, over the whole playground, like a giant bird of prey – dark and menacing. I looked up, but there was nothing there.

When I looked down again, I saw that Anna was staring at me. She held out her hand. I opened my own hand and let go of the rest of the gravel. It stayed where it was as I took Anna's hand.

'What's happening?'

'It's *him*. That's what you can feel. Like you've been punched.'

The tiny stones hung in the air behind us as we barged through the door and into the main reception area.

'Midnight is coming,' she said. 'Run!'

• CHAPTER FOUR •

'Maybe we should split up,' I suggested breathlessly as we ran down the Maths corridor.

'Split up? That wouldn't help,' Anna assured me.

'Just a thought,' I muttered.

I could see Mr Anderson poised by the whiteboard, in the process of writing an equation or something – a jumble of letters and numbers and signs. His pen was stuck at the end of a '3'. There were several older children spilling out of M7, just poised in mid-step. They must have been kept in, or their lesson had overrun. One boy was laughing – his mirth caught in a three-dimensional photo. We dodged round them and they ignored us. Didn't move.

'But if it's just him . . .'

'It isn't. He's never alone.'

I pushed open the door at the end of the corridor. Once we were through, it snapped straight back to where it had been before, slightly ajar. We were now in the Art block.

'He was alone when I saw him the other evening.'

'No, he wasn't.' Anna was looking through the glass in the door of the ceramics room. There was a class in there, working through the break to empty the kiln. 'Maybe we can hide in here,' she said. 'We can't keep running from him. Not for ever.' She pushed the door open. 'And I do mean *for ever*,' she added solemnly.

There was another door at the back, leading into one of the Art rooms. A third door gave into the back corridor, which led to a fire escape and the English department. So at least we had other exits to run for. We pushed our way through the pupils to get to the other side of the room. Like the doors, they moved for us, then immediately clicked back to where they had been.

'They'll get a shock if he starts time up again with us here,' Anna said drily.

'You mean he can just start and stop time, like a clock?'

She paused to make a point of looking round the frozen room, finishing with a glare at me. 'What do you think?' We ducked down behind a workbench on the far side of the room. 'He can stop it, start it, speed it up, slow it down. Though no one caught inside would ever notice of course.' She tapped in annoyance at the black watch she was wearing. 'Stopped,' she murmured. She didn't seem surprised. 'I can get it working again. But that won't help you . . .'

'So how come we can tell time has stopped?' I wanted to know. 'How come we can move about?'

'I'm trained,' she said, and there was a hint of pride in her voice as she said it. 'And you . . . Well.' She shrugged.

'I know, I'm lost.'

'It's not just the world he can affect,' Anna

said, and I was surprised to hear the tremor in her voice. I realised, perhaps for the first time, that she was actually frightened. 'It's people too. Or anything. He can rewind your own time, or speed it up. He can freeze you into a coma for ever while the world goes on around you. Or he can make you a baby again. Or –' her voice was quiet and shaking, '– he can age you so fast that you wither and die and crumble to dust in a minute. Even people who don't exist inside time. Like us.'

This sounded ridiculous, but I knew she was telling the truth. It was no more ridiculous than so many things that were happening.

'What's he *want* with us?' I wondered.

'I don't know, but I think he wants *you*.'

'Me?'

Her voice was high-pitched and tight with nerves. 'All right – you ask him.'

I actually considered this. I mean, I didn't know – I only had Anna's word to go by, and a brief conversation with the man. But I could tell how scared she was, so I asked, 'What did you mean, he's never alone?'

'There are creatures with him,' she said, looking round the whole time – as if they might already be creeping up on us. 'They're always there, with Midnight. We call them Skitters.'

'Skitters?'

She nodded. 'Skitters. Because you have to concentrate to even catch a glimpse of them as they flit between the now and the then. They flicker in and out of real time, so they can't usually be seen by ordinary people.'

I thought about the vague shadows I had seen with Midnight. 'What do they look like?'

'Depends where and when he found them. Just keep out of their way, right? They'll try to catch you, to take you to him. That's if they don't rip you apart themselves, just for the fun of it.' She shuddered.

There was a breeze. I could feel it on my cheek and I could see it riffling through stray strands of Anna's hair. She nodded and put her finger to her lips. Her face seemed drained of colour – Midnight was here.

The door to the ceramics room crashed open. I leaned across, to peer round the end of the workbench where we were sheltering, but Anna grabbed my arm, shaking her head urgently. So I stayed put. But I couldn't help wondering what Midnight was doing. Was he standing in the doorway, looking round the room? Had he gone, moved on down the corridor to the next classroom? Or was he walking slowly towards us, about to appear round the workbench at any moment, silver-topped cane raised and ready to strike? I strained to hear any footsteps.

'It's no use hiding.' His voice echoed in the room, as if the whole place was empty. I could hear the amusement, like he was talking to stupid kids who'd hidden in the most obvious place and left their feet sticking out. But we hadn't. He must be bluffing.

'That workbench was put there just over three years ago,' he went on. 'I can see the room as it was before the bench was there. And I can see it as it is now. So I can see you, girl. Quite clearly.'

'Can he?' I mouthed anxiously at Anna.

Her face was pale, resigned. Anyway, however he did it, he knew exactly where we were. So I stood up.

'We meet again, young man,' Midnight said, as Anna and I appeared above the level of the workbench.

He was standing just inside the doorway. And as Anna had told me, he was not alone. Was it my imagination, or were the shadows round him deeper than they should be? Were there shapes, movements – *creatures* – within those shadows? I didn't waste time trying to tell – I was more concerned with the nightmare creature I *could* see.

In one hand Midnight was holding his cane, as if it was a long magician's wand. In the other he held the end of a leash. And the leash was attached to the spiked collar of the most ferocious-looking animal I had ever seen. It was straining towards us so hard its front paws were almost off the ground, but Midnight effortlessly held the creature back.

'What is it?' I gasped.

Its shape was familiar. It was like a tiger, except that its fur was matted and coarse and the head was a different shape, built round a jutting mouth full of teeth. Teeth that were angled viciously outwards. Blood-red eyes glared malevolently at us and a string of saliva dripped from one of the yellowed fangs.

'Sabre-toothed tiger,' I murmured, remembering it from pictures.

'What?' Anna said quietly.

'It's a prehistoric animal,' I protested, my mouth dry and my legs shaking with fear. 'It doesn't exist.'

'Of course it exists,' Anna said. 'Just not in this time.'

'She's right,' Midnight conceded happily. 'As I can demonstrate quite simply.' He gave a gentle tug on the leash and the animal turned to look at him. 'Not the boy,' Midnight said. 'I need him.'

Beside me, Anna gasped and took a step backwards. In front of me, Midnight leaned forward and unclipped the leash from the animal's collar.

The beast's mouth opened wide in a savage snarl of anticipation and it padded slowly towards us across the room. Slowly at first, then more quickly, weaving between the frozen children, faster and faster, claws clicking on the bare wooden floor. Then it was running at full speed, launching itself from its hind legs, flying towards us, front paws outstretched, teeth bared, snarling and snapping.

I shoved Anna aside, I don't know why. Midnight had said I was safe for now. Call it instinct, or bravery, or probably just stupidity. I pushed her roughly out of the way and leaped in between her falling body and the massive animal.

'No!' I heard someone shout – a voice full of anger and determination. My own voice, I realised. I was reaching out, mirroring the tiger, ready to grab its outstretched legs and wrestle with it. Ready, I suppose, to die. The point of a claw reached my arm as the creature flew at me.

It stopped – frozen in mid-air like the skipping girl outside.

Anna was crawling away, pulling herself to her feet, fiddling desperately with the watch at her wrist.

Midnight was swinging his cane so that the silver end slapped into the palm of his other hand as he watched. The cane froze too, but his face twisted into a snarl of anger almost like the tiger's.

'More powerful than I thought,' he hissed.

'What happened?' I blurted out. A few inches in front of me, a dribble of saliva hung from the jaws of the tiger, like an icicle. I stepped back and helped Anna to her feet. 'How did you do that?'

She shook her head, equally amazed. 'I didn't,' she said.

But I barely heard her. I was still staring at the sabre-toothed tiger hanging impossibly in the air. Watching the fur fade and sag, the bones becoming visible through its flank. The head was becoming a skull – bone yellowing and cracking. For a moment a skeleton reached out towards us, like we were on a ghost train. Then it crashed down on to the workbench, bones shattering and crumbling to dust.

Anna said quietly, 'I've never seen that happen before.'

'Why did it crumble like that?'

She stared at me like I was completely daft. 'Because it's so old. A fossil. Prehistoric. Think how you'll look in a million years.'

There wasn't time to discuss it. Midnight too had been surprised, and stood watching me in something close to astonishment. But now the air round Midnight, the shadows in the doorway, seemed to swirl and thicken and solidify. Shapes were forming – shapes of things that I instinctively knew had been there all the time, if only I could have seen them. They flickered in and out of reality so that looking at them was like watching a badly tuned television. Imps or gargoyles, I don't know which they reminded me of more – grotesque, tiny figures with stubby horns on their stone-like heads and leathery wings. I caught a glimpse of a forked tail as glowing red eyes stared out at us from the evil, angry faces.

Three of the figures crouched round Midnight, like children with their father. Midnight patted one gently on the head. Then he stretched out a hand to point at me and Anna. His fingers snapped, a sudden echoing sound in the empty room full of people.

The Skitters flapped their wings and I could see the leather-like fabric of the skin pull taut as they rose slowly into the air. Their bony fingers clicked and clutched in anticipation as they started towards us.

Again, I pushed Anna aside, but more gently this time.

'No,' she said. 'They aren't real, not like the tiger. These are from outside time altogether. Age has no meaning – you can't stop them.'

As if to prove the point, one of the creatures whipped between us, cackling with laughter as dry and ugly as its wings. I saw its face close up as I pulled away – a glimpse of peeling, layered skin like weather-damaged stonework. Like an old statue. Then I was falling backwards, out of the way as another of the Skitters flew past.

'Run, Jamie!' Anna was shouting. 'Run!'

She was already scrambling towards the nearest door out of the room, slamming it back at the Skitter as she raced through. The door caught the thing in mid-air and smacked into it with a crunch. Then the Skitter was up again and through the door – the wood splintering and cracking and falling apart round it like dry old leaves. I could see Anna running across the adjoining room, weaving between desks and pupils. The Skitter's wings beat ponderously as it followed. And the door slowly faded back to how it had been – intact and unblemished.

The two other creatures were between me and the door. So I turned and ran the other way – vaulted over the workbench, crashed past children, sent pots and vases flying. But they simply flickered back to where they had been as I passed.

'Bring him back to me, my beauties,' Midnight called from behind me as I ran. He was laughing. 'Let's see how clever you *really* are, Jamie Grant. How useful to us.'

Yes, I thought, let's see. I could feel the breeze from the wings of the Skitters ruffling my hair and I quickened my pace. I crashed through the door into the corridor beyond. If I could get to the fire escape, there was a chance. Just a slim chance . . .

The creatures flapped their wings desperately, but they were heavy and ponderous and I was able to get away from them, widening the gap. Somehow, though, I knew that while I would soon be out of breath, they wouldn't tire. There was just one hope in my mind – that I could get out onto the playground ahead of them.

Along the corridor and down the fire escape. I was behind the English block now, close to the bike sheds. Round to the playground – quick! The door opened again behind me, the only sound in the still world.

I watched the Skitters emerge from behind the English block. They hung in the air, wings beating slowly and noisily like bellows. They seemed confused, turning slowly as they surveyed the playground – staring at the hundreds of children frozen in the middle of what they were doing. Right in the middle of the silent crowd, I stood as still as death and looked back at them defiantly.

Although I knew that no time was passing, it still seemed to last for ever. I wondered how Anna was doing – had she escaped? Would I ever see her again? I hoped so, and not just because, apart from her, I was now completely alone in the world.

Midnight stepped out behind his minions and I felt cold. He stared across the playground, seeming to fix his attention on each child in turn.

I had chosen an awkward stance, trying to look as though I had been in mid-step when time ground to a halt. Now I was paying for it. My leg ached and I longed to rub it, to move, to ease my muscles . . .

Could he tell who was frozen in time and who was just pretending? Or was it possible that Midnight couldn't see it was me in the middle of the crowd? Was I somehow immune to his evil eye, to his ability to see through time itself. Did I really have some power, like Anna had said? I remembered what had happened to the tiger and hoped it meant I had a chance at least.

The ache in my leg was unbearable. I was going to have to move soon, and then it wouldn't matter if he could see through my act. Could I outrun Midnight and the creatures? And if so, where would I run to? I had nowhere to go. I had to find Anna – and she could be anywhere. Any*when*.

I was bracing myself, ready to run, when Midnight gave a snarl of rage and turned away. Perhaps he'd decided I'd gone another way. I heard the click of his fingers as he called the creatures off. They spun lazily in the air and flew slowly after him, out of sight.

With a heartfelt sigh of relief I stretched. I tried to rub some feeling back into my tortured leg and hobbled off quickly towards the drive. There were only two places where I *could* go, I decided. Only two places where I might find Anna. If she was still alive. One was home, where, if nothing else, I could perhaps talk to Ellie when she got back from her school. The other was the road outside, where I had seen Anna yesterday. Where she said the time break would be. Would she be there now, waiting for it?

The traffic was frozen like a photograph. Spray from a puddle hung in the air round the stationary car wheel that had sent it flying. A cyclist balanced impossibly upright, head low over the handlebars.

I stopped at the gates and went to look at my watch, then realised how pointless that was. So instead I looked back at the school – at the children laughing silently and playing without moving. But there *was* movement. Inside the school, behind a window in the main block

I could see a figure looking back at me. It was Midnight.

I swallowed, turned and ran across the road.

The moment I stepped off the pavement, there was noise. Laughter and shouting, a plane somewhere high above, traffic. Then screeching brakes. Cars hurtling towards me. Spray from a puddle splashing over my feet as I stared in horrified disbelief at the car heading straight for me.

TIME RUNNERS

• CHAPTER FIVE •

I leaped out of the way, tripping on the kerb and falling backwards. The world seemed to slow momentarily – the cars whizzing past blurred like brush marks in wet paint. Then they were back to full speed, a horn blaring, drivers still braking as they worked out what was happening.

Some daft kid, almost running out in the road. Almost.

I walked to the crossing, my head in a spin from everything. Was Anna all right? Was Midnight coming after me or was I safe now? What could I do? Where could I go?

The time break, as Anna had called it, was just opening above the pavement. At the point where

I had dropped my rucksack the day before with Anna. She was right. I knew straight away what it was. It looked like when it's very hot and the air sort of shimmers, or it seems like there's a puddle in the road and there isn't. That's what it was like. Except it was shimmering in the air above the pavement, and the edges were like broken glass – a window out of reality.

You know those funny pictures where it looks like a spiky pattern of colour, but if you stare at it and try to focus at a point behind the picture you see something else? Like a three-dimensional image of a dinosaur or a train or a face. You can stare for ages and see nothing but the mess of colour, and then suddenly the picture is there and you can't imagine how you ever missed it, but you daren't look away or even blink in case it goes again.

That's what it was like looking through the broken air. I could see the street continuing beyond, stretching out towards home. But there was an unreal quality to it, a lack of depth and focus. And when I blinked and looked again, I was aware of the broken edges, like shattered

69

glass. And then, slowly, I could see another picture overlaid on the window, on the tear.

Someone walked past. A woman with a pushchair. A tiny hand was poking out from the pushchair as they went by, waving a small board book attached to the buggy by a coiled string like you see on old phones.

I nearly called out. But it was too late. They walked right through the time break. The air shimmered and warped, as if they had passed through a thin layer of water. Then it settled back into shape and now the picture was clearer than ever.

Mother and child, walking through an unreal landscape, like they were on a television screen, gradually fading from sight, disappearing from the world in a swirling mass of colour. Waves of light crashing onto the beach at the edge of our world. Washing their way in, breaking through. I could see that with every swell and fade of colour, whenever the light grabbed and tore at the edges of the hole in time, it grew wider and somehow deeper too, as if I was looking down a tunnel with glass walls. Growing. How big would it get?

'Unless we stop it, it will get bigger and deeper and stronger,' Anna said, suddenly beside me. 'It will swallow everything that's in its way. Like it swallowed them.'

'What's happened to them?' I asked, my throat dry and my voice croaking.

'Nothing. They never existed. They've gone. And unless we can stop it, unless we can sort things out, they will never have existed. Like you.'

Anna took my hand in hers and together we stared at the swirling colours. I held on tight.

'How do we stop it?' I asked.

'By finding out how it started, what made it happen. Then we stop that. It's the only way to undo the damage being done.'

'But it's already happened. You said so – the step off the path that eventually leads to the cliff. And here we are, on the brink, about to walk off the edge.'

'I told you. This is the end of the journey. We need to retrace our steps, *time's* steps, and find out where it first went wrong. Put it back on track. Somehow.'

We turned slowly to look at each other, still holding hands. Aware that all we had left in this world was each other.

'They were just the first,' Anna said. 'The woman and her child. As it gets stronger it will suck more and more things in. Things and people.'

'And then what?'

She shrugged.

'I'm glad you're safe,' I said.

'Once I was far enough from Midnight I could dial out.'

'You could what?'

She tapped her watch, like that meant something. 'It's hard to get away from Skitters. But I've had lots of practice.'

'They scared the hell out of me.'

'Me too,' she admitted quietly. 'And they only have to catch you once. Once is for ever.'

'So, what now?'

'It's so weak, so new,' she said thoughtfully staring at the hole in the air. 'Like whatever caused it has only just happened. Neat trick with that tiger, by the way.'

'Thanks. I don't know what I did, or how I did it.'

'Instinct. You'll learn how to control it. We all have some power, though not as much as you. We all learn how to use what we have. Training.'

She turned away, and I wondered if there was a time academy or school or something I'd have to go to. first lesson: how to fossilize a tiger. Then after break it's double Clockwork before History. Or something.

There was a shape forming within the colours. A dark smudge in the light. Growing deeper and more solid as we watched.

'It's a rare skill you have,' Anna said. She was watching the shape form too. 'Maybe unique. That's probably why . . .'

'Why I'm lost?'

'Why Midnight wants you.' She nodded at the rupture in reality.

And I could see now that the dark shape *was* Midnight. Stepping out into the real world in front of us. There was no sign of the Skitters, but I knew they were there. I could feel them, sense them, almost smell them.

The traffic went by, the people walked and talked and laughed, the whistle blew for the end of break. The world went on oblivious as Midnight stepped out of the time break in front of us.

'I underestimated you,' he said. He was looking straight at me. Like Anna didn't even exist – and that annoyed me.

'What do you want?' I wasn't frightened this time, just angry.

'I want you,' he said. He was smiling, but it was a humourless, frozen sort of smile and his voice was cold. 'I want the power you so obviously have.'

Behind Midnight, I could see other shapes now. Writhing, clawing, scrabbling at the edges of the rip in time. Had they been drawn here by his presence? Had he brought them with him or had they found it on their own? Could they escape into the real world? I shivered at the thought.

Anna was backing away, tugging at my school blazer. 'Don't let him touch you.'

Midnight spared her a glance, no more. For that

second, the smile was gone. Then he switched it on again and turned back to me. 'You're very special, you know. Very special indeed. I can use someone like you.'

'And he means "use",' Anna murmured.

'Not interested,' I said, trying to sound as cold as he did.

'You've not heard my offer yet.'

'Still not interested.'

He sighed. 'Shame. Perhaps I can persuade you to change your mind.' He curled his fingers into a half-fist and inspected the nails carefully. 'After all, we do have some time.' He looked up at me, eyes as hard and dark as coal. 'All the time in the world, in fact.'

As he spoke, he circled slowly round. Anna and I were backing away, but it was like the laws of geography as well as the laws of time had changed around me. Somehow he was the other side of us, and we were between him and the shimmering hole in the world. We were so close I could hear it rumbling and growling, like a hungry animal.

'Don't get too near,' Anna warned me. 'Don't

get sucked in. No one can survive falling through a time break.'

Midnight coughed, dusting his free hand on the lapel of his dark coat. The other hand twirled the cane nonchalantly. 'I think you'll find that's "*almost* no one",' he said with false modesty. 'If you're powerful enough you'll survive. Trapped outside time for all eternity, of course, unless you can learn how to move through the fifth and sixth dimensions. Or unless you have a friend who can . . .' He raised an eyebrow and took a step towards Anna.

She gave a little cry of alarm and stepped aside, careful to keep well back from the time break.

Midnight clicked his tongue. 'Thought not. Such a shame. Such a great shame. Perhaps you'll reconsider my offer in a moment or two, when you've seen what can happen.' He was talking to me, but looking at Anna. He raised the cane suddenly, like it was a weapon. Which, I suddenly realised, it was.

A line of blue fire spat from the end of the cane and roared towards Anna. It thumped into her chest and knocked her off her feet – sending her flying backwards towards the shimmering hole.

Again time slowed for me. But not enough – not nearly enough. I couldn't reach her, couldn't save her. Instead I dived backwards, towards the time break. Hoping to block it, to get there before Anna tumbled and fell. She had almost recovered her balance, but was being dragged backwards, pulled off her feet again like she was falling, but sideways.

I reached the jagged edge of the hole just as Anna did. I grabbed her, held her, felt her close and warm – felt her fear and the frantic beating of her heart. Felt the pull as I too was dragged in. I pushed with all my might, sending Anna sprawling away.

But the effort of pushing her away forced me backwards another step. A step too far. It was as if a hundred hands had grabbed me from behind. I was yanked off my feet and hurtled backwards with a cry of anger, of fear – and of triumph as I saw Anna getting to her feet and looking at me, sad and afraid. But she was all right.

The sharp edges of the hole in reality tore through me like broken glass as I fell. Dark shapes closed in around me. The swirl and roar were blotted out by the sound of Midnight's laughter as the blackness closed over me and I tumbled downwards into oblivion.

CHAPTER SIX

🕐 No Time At All

I might have been there for a split second. Or I might have been there for years. I had no way of knowing. I was in utter blackness. I could almost hear the silence, it was so complete. I tried shouting, at least I think I did. Nothing. I stared so hard into the darkness that I could see shapes that weren't there, like when you close your eyes after looking at a bright light.

Maybe I dreamed.

Then someone walked across the darkness and I realised I was standing in a room. A completely black room – so black I couldn't see where the ceiling or the floor joined the walls.

It was a man. Or something that looked like a man. He was tall and thin and wearing a grey cloak. The edges of the cloak were lost in the darkness of the surroundings, and his pale face was shadowed beneath a hood. He was walking slowly towards me, though because his feet were hidden by his cloak and the floor was invisibly black, it seemed more like he was floating.

'That wasn't terribly clever,' he said as he approached. His voice was cracked and dry and his face, now I could see it, was wrinkled and ancient. He threw back the hood of his cloak and I saw that he was almost bald. A few last wisps of fine white hair clung to the sides of his weathered, blotchy scalp.

'Sorry,' I replied, as much to check my voice was working again as anything. 'Where am I?' I asked when I found that it did.

He smiled. It was a kindly smile – unlike Midnight's. 'Nowhere. Nowhere at all. Not yet. You fell into the time break, don't you remember?'

I nodded. 'Where's Anna? Is she all right?'

He seemed to consider this carefully, though his reply gave no hint that he had even heard the question: 'You were lucky. If you were any less powerful, we might never have found you. As it is you've been here for quite a while. Years. We lose a lot of Runners that way. You . . . You must be exceptional to have survived at all, let alone for so long. So very long.'

'Runners? What do you mean?'

'Come,' he said. 'I will show you.' He held out his hand.

It was like taking hold of a bundle of old sticks, dry and brittle. But his grip was firm. And suddenly the room was full of bright sunlight and the air smelled of the sea and we were somewhere else.

🕐 21st June 1724

It was a huge room, with a long wooden table running the length of it. Beyond the table, stone archways gave out on to a view of a bay. Or the sea. An expanse of glittering water, anyway, with the sun shining down on it from a clear blue sky. The buildings shimmered in reflection. It was a scene I knew, though I had never been there before. It looked like a painting, only from the wrong angle.

Sitting at the table was Anna. As soon as she saw me she leaped to her feet. She glanced at the old man, as if for permission, before running across the room and hugging me tightly.

'You're here!' she exclaimed excitedly. 'I told them you'd be here. I knew Senex would find you.'

'Yes,' I said, confused and dazed by it all. 'I'm here. Wherever . . .'

'We are in Venice,' the old man – Senex – said. 'In the year 1724.'

He led me over to the table. I sat down, facing the glittering water outside.

'We have to keep moving,' Senex explained. 'Otherwise they would find us. It is a risk to be in the same time and place more than once. That would be playing into our enemies' hands.'

'Your enemies?'

'You have met one of them.'

'Midnight,' Anna said. She was sitting further down the table. Smiling. I smiled back. Somehow, here I felt safe.

'Oh, yeah,' I said. 'Him.'

'I gather you gave him something to think about,' Senex told me. He had taken his place at the head of the table. Perhaps he was less impressed by the view. Or used to it.

I shrugged. 'S'pose so. We got away, anyhow.'

'No false modesty,' he observed. 'But no arrogance or pride either. That's good. Yes,' he went on, nodding slowly, 'I think you will make an excellent Runner.'

He'd mentioned 'Runners' before. 'So what is a Runner?' I turned to Anna. 'Are you a Runner?'

Anna was quiet, looking at Senex. The old man gathered his thoughts, his fingers tapping lightly on the surface of the table as he considered. 'We belong to a group – an Alliance gathered from all periods, all places. Some of us have positions of authority within the Alliance, and we have the responsibility of seeing that time itself remains intact and on course. Uncorrupted. Safe. For the day-to-day, moment-to-moment work to this end, we employ the Runners.'

'Like policemen,' Anna put in. 'Troops on the ground.'

'With this Alliance in charge?'

'Something like that,' Senex agreed. 'We send the Runners to points in history where there is or will be or has been a problem. Runners usually work in pairs — an adult and a child. The adult provides experience and logic and analysis, while the child has an instinctive understanding of time. Anna here is particularly useful —' he nodded towards her and she smiled, '— as she is between the two. She is gaining the experience of an adult, while still retaining the intuition of the child.'

'Being stuck at fourteen has its uses,' she murmured. 'I've been fourteen for years,' she added with a touch of sadness.

Senex seemed not to notice. 'Most Runners,' he was saying, 'have the ability to manipulate time or to interact with it. The more experienced and versed and talented the Runner, the greater their powers. Some have the ability to rewind and replay events, some can stop time in a moment while they move round inside it ...'

'Like Midnight,' I said.

'Like Midnight,' Senex agreed. 'Although he is exceptional, what we call an *Adept*. Someone who – either through instinct or training – has a very powerful control over time itself. Even for an Adept, Midnight is tremendously gifted.' Senex cleared his throat. 'But I think that is quite enough information to be going on with for now. You have work to do.'

'Work?'

'Anna's mission, her "Run", as we call it, was to discover the cause of the time distortion that you fell into and close the time break before any permanent damage is done.'

'Is it something to do with me being lost?' I asked.

Senex stood up and walked towards the arched wall, and Anna and I followed. The view out over the water was magnificent and the sun was a warm orange disc in the azure sky.

'You were lost because you fell through time,' Anna said.

'Don't be daft,' I told her. 'I didn't fall into the time break thing until after I was lost.'

Senex sighed. 'You must forget everything you know about cause and effect, about the order in which you think things must happen. Just because you had not yet experienced it does not mean it hadn't happened.' He didn't wait for me to try to work this out, but went on: 'Now, Anna tells me you have considerable talents,' he said.

'Eh?'

'What you did with the tiger, and the fact that you escaped from Midnight,' Anna explained.

'Oh, that. I suppose.'

'At the moment you do not understand what you can do or how you do it,' Senex said. 'But you will learn.' He turned to face me. The light was behind him now as he stood framed in the arch. His face was shadow and his form silhouette – like when I first saw him. 'To discover and harness your power,' he went on, 'to be an Adept – if that is what you are destined to become – you will need to learn how to use that power.'

'And you say Midnight is an Adept?' I asked, wondering how he fitted in with the plans and aspirations of this Alliance.

'Darkling Midnight is many things,' Senex said quietly. 'Be wary of him, young man. He knows who you are now, and he does not take kindly to being crossed.'

'And he isn't part of this Alliance?'

'He's a *Dark* Runner,' Anna said. She was sitting on the long wooden table, kicking her legs back and forth. 'One of the Dark Assembly. He wants to recruit you to help *them*.'

'There are Adepts on both sides,' Senex explained. 'Although very few of them. Not many are that gifted. When a new Adept is discovered, both sides – the Alliance and the Dark Assembly – naturally try to recruit them.'

'And what do they want? What are they up to?'

'They seek to disrupt and destroy time and reality,' Senex said seriously. 'The Dark Assembly sends its own agents into history – to exploit and create problems. Some, like Midnight, may once have been human. Others . . .' He shook his head. 'Others may be what you would term ghosts, shadows, wraiths, gargoyles . . . The Runners call them Skitters, and they exist on the very edge of human consciousness, poking through into reality.'

It was quiet for a while. Anna sat on the table and kicked her legs, Senex turned back to admire the view.

'But . . .' I said hesitantly. 'I mean, why? Why do they want to cause trouble?'

'Just because they do,' Anna said. 'They're vandals, hooligans. They do it because they can.'

Senex held up his hand to stop her. 'It's easy to dismiss them as just troublemakers,' he said. 'But there is a purpose to it. A twisted, insane purpose, but a deliberate plan nonetheless.'

'Which is?' I prompted.

Senex sighed, and I got the impression it was a point of view he had explained many times. 'They believe they are creating a better world. A better history,' he told us. 'They believe that the ends justify the means. They would tear down existing history so as to create a new history to take its place. If you ask Midnight, I have no doubt he will tell you he is on the side of angels. He would tell you what he does is better in the long term. He is creating a version of history where there is less suffering, fewer wars, no hatred or avoidable death . . .'

'Doesn't sound so bad,' I said.

'No, it doesn't,' Senex agreed. 'But there is a price to be paid. To save one poor child who would die in a needless war, Midnight would change events so that a thousand other innocent children are never born. He would deny them life, and claim he is making a better world.'

'Not so good,' I agreed.

'And perhaps worse than that,' Senex said quietly, 'he would remove from people the very things that make them human. He would take away the choice – the freedom to make their own decisions. Free will. He would impose an order for the good of everyone, and with the agreement of no one. The will and vision of the Dark Assembly imposed on everyone throughout all of history and for evermore. *That*,' Senex told me, 'is what we oppose.'

Explained like that, it didn't sound such a great idea any more. I stood there wondering what happened next. Eventually I summoned up enough courage to ask, though I wasn't sure I wanted to know the answer. 'So,' I said slowly, 'what now?'

'Anna has a job to do,' Senex said in answer to my question. He did not turn from the view out over Venice.

Anna jumped down from the table. She seemed keen to leave right away and I felt a bit sad that she was so ready to abandon me.

'What about me?'

'As I said, Anna is becoming as experienced as an adult as well as the instinctive child she remains at heart. Now that her partner is no longer . . . available, thanks to the intervention of Midnight, she will need a replacement. Someone she can work with. And this time the Alliance has decided that Anna is ready to take on the responsibility of looking after someone less experienced than herself. Starting their training.'

Anna was grinning. She knew already, I realised, as the implications of Senex's words slowly sank in. 'You mean *me*?'

'We're going back,' said Anna. 'Welcome to the Alliance!'

CHAPTER SEVEN

🕐 11TH OCTOBER (AGAIN)

So here I am, back home. Or rather, standing on the path outside school where the time break will be. And Anna is with me. It's the day before I was lost, and in the real world we haven't even met yet. Except I'm lost already – once it happens, it's for always. If we sort out the time break, we could get the mother and child back – and anyone else who fell into it. But not me. Because I've already become part of the events that led to the time break being fixed. I have to stay lost for that to happen. Trouble with time is, it messes with your head.

'Can people see me?' I wonder.

91

'Of course they can.'

'But, if I've been lost . . .'

'They can see me, can't they? *You* can see me.'

I pretended to look round in surprise. 'Who said that?!' She wasn't impressed. So I got right to the question I really wanted to ask. 'Mum and Dad . . .'

She nodded. 'Yeah. They can see you, just like they can see me. The Alliance can put us back into time, but just as people, not as who we once were. So no one will recognise us – not even our own parents. Not any more. To them, you're just a boy.'

'But if we're back in time . . .'

She smiled at my use of words. 'Back?'

'Whatever.' I wasn't smiling, I just wanted to understand. There were rules, but they weren't ones I knew. 'I just mean that we can change things. They don't have to be the same.'

'It's not that easy.'

We had started walking. Heading towards home. Would Mum be there? I checked my watch.

Only it wasn't my watch. It was smaller, little

more than a flat black disc marked off with Roman numerals. The date was printed in full across the circular face. It was identical to the watch Anna was wearing.

'That's so you know when we are,' she explained. 'And you can use it to find the Alliance, if you need them. Ways out and in, that sort of thing. I'll show you later.'

'It's the day before yesterday,' I said, pointing to the date on the watch. 'And we haven't met yet. So why can't we change things?'

'Because you know they've already happened.'

I wasn't convinced. 'You changed the photo,' I said. 'I know how you did it now. You used this.' I held up my hand and waved the watch at her. 'You used it to go back to when the photo was taken so you were in it. Didn't you?'

'What if I did?'

'Then you changed things.'

We were turning into the close now, and I began to wonder at the back of my mind what I'd say to Mum. She would expect me to be at school still. I *was* at school still – sort of.

'Like I said, it isn't easy.' Anna stopped and

I waited for her to go on. 'You get one shot at it. When you go back.'

'Back?'

She glared, but I was joking – repeating her own word to her. 'You can go back and change something, so long as you weren't a part of it in the first place. That day, when the photo was taken, that was nothing to do with me. I hadn't been there before. So I could go and change things. I could stand in front of the camera and have my picture taken. But I couldn't go there again and do something else. I couldn't jump up at the back of the same group and be in the picture twice. It doesn't work like that. You can change other people's history, but never your own. I was there, so I'm a part of it. That bit of history is set in concrete as far as I'm concerned. Understand?'

'No.' Again, I sort of got the gist of it, but understand? No way. Not then. But I tried. 'So you can't go and save your friend. The guy that Midnight clobbered.'

She winced, at either the memory or my description of it. Or maybe both. 'No,' she agreed. 'I was already there and I didn't save him. Not then, not now, not ever.'

'Even though it hasn't happened yet?'

She lost it then, yelling at me, eyes blazing and angry: 'It *has* happened, don't you get it? You still don't see that? It has happened – it's happened to *me*! It doesn't matter whether it's yesterday, today or tomorrow, I was there. Will be there, am there now. I didn't, won't, *can't* stop it. It happened.' She turned away. 'Live with it,' I heard her mutter. '*I* have to.'

I put my hand on her shoulder. 'Sorry. You're right, I don't get it. But I am trying.'

She turned and made an effort to smile back at me.

'Hey,' I said, 'we're going to be such a team!'

'Going to be?' she said, that half-smile back in place.

'Can I see Mum?' I asked. 'Can I at least warn her what's going to happen to me? It is the past, after all,' I pointed out.

But Anna wasn't impressed. 'It wouldn't do any good. She'd say you should be in school. Or she might not even remember you. You may not have fallen into the time break yet, but time is already falling apart. The longer we wait, the worse the effects will get. Remember that woman and the kid in the pushchair. There will be others by now. More all the time.'

'But that's . . .' I struggled to think of a word. 'Crazy,' I decided. 'You went back and got in the picture. I can go back and change things in the same way. I must be able to.' A thought occurred to me, an idea so obvious I couldn't believe I'd not thought of it before. 'I can warn myself not to fall into the time break,' I exclaimed. 'I can stop myself from ever being lost in the first place!'

But from Anna's expression I guessed it didn't work that way. I felt the bottom fall away from my stomach, but I knew that I was still determined to try.

I told Anna I always come out late, so we waited behind the science block while the other children streamed out of school. How I envied them – going about as if nothing was different, nothing was wrong. The biggest worry any of them might have would be getting homework done, or avoiding Bill Hablish on the way home, or what their mum would cook for tea . . .

I knew I would run a mile if I saw myself coming. Talk about freaked out – it wouldn't do any good to frighten myself off without delivering the warning. And from what Anna said, I couldn't have spoken to myself anyway – that would be changing my own history and time won't let you do that. She wasn't happy, but eventually Anna agreed to do it.

'I'll be out in a minute,' I said.

I must have sounded impatient or tetchy, because Anna tutted. 'I know. I won't miss you.' She waited a moment longer, then said, 'Not going to tell me what I should say, then? Again?'

'Sorry,' I mumbled. 'I'm just . . .'

'I know. It's all right. I'll do what I can.' Then she was gone, striding out across the tarmac towards the driveway that led to the main school gates.

And there I was. I ducked into the shadows at the side of the building and watched myself – head down, rucksack hooked over one shoulder, in a world of my own while the rest of the world stopped for Anna. I saw myself glance at Anna and walk on.

She called out. I heard her: 'Jamie!'

And I saw myself look round, not knowing who had spoken. 'Twerp,' I muttered aloud, amused but sad at the thought ... And at the memory, as I realised what was going to happen. After all, it had already happened.

On the driveway, my other self was talking to Anna, frowning, making a point of looking at my watch. I glanced at the watch I had now – the thin black dial ... Was this really only two days ago? Anna was right, it had no meaning. Two days or a lifetime. Same thing.

Then Anna glanced back at me. It was an 'I told you so' look, and I mouthed, 'Go on!' at her. I doubt she could see. Already I was feeling depressed and annoyed with myself – myself then for not listening, and myself now for being so helpless.

My then self looked over, following Anna's gaze, and I stepped back into the darkest shadows. Anna was talking again. But I didn't think it would do any good. She glanced over at me once more, and I could recall myself, standing there, watching her looking at the science block – at me, although I didn't know it at the time.

Then, abruptly, my other self seemed to give up on the conversation. Turned and walked off towards the gates. I just stared. Gutted. Empty inside – my last hope, however slim, gone. Like Anna said – for ever.

'Be kind to Ellie!' Anna shouted after him. The then me. 'You'll need her.'

Then-me didn't even pause. Just kept walking, head down. Anna watched all the way to the gate. She shook her head and turned back to me – the real me, the *now* me.

At the gate the then me glanced at his/my watch, looked back at Anna, turned and walked away.

'And so it goes. Just as it did before.' Anna shrugged. 'You'll go out and post the letters later this evening. You'll meet Midnight and see me again – except that for me it will be the first time.'

'I can't stop it,' I said sadly.

'No.'

We were sitting on the cracked bench in the bus stop on the Cavershall Road. It was getting dark. Buses and people came and went. We sat there. And further along the street, the air shimmered and rippled. More people disappeared into the time break – a man and his dog, a woman out jogging. The edges were clipping the side of the street. Soon they reached the cycle lane between the pavement and the main part of the road. The first cyclist swerved round it, as if sensing there was something there. Others were not so lucky . . .

'So, what can we do?' I asked, as another cyclist pedalled into nowhere.

'We have to close the time break, otherwise it will continue to stretch and grow and everyone will fall into it.'

'Everyone?' I echoed.

'Possibly. All history will change, and the people change with it. Remember the woman and her child – they just don't exist in the history that's being created. There will be others like that. Millions of them.'

'How do we sort it out, then?'

'We have to find the trigger – the event or moment or person or thing that caused the break to come into existence.'

'So we need to be there to see what happens when it starts to form?'

'We have to be there,' she agreed. 'And it may not seem like it, but the longer we hang around here, the worse it gets. The harder it will be.'

I stood up to stretch my legs. My bum was getting sore from the hard seat. It was getting dark outside the bus shelter, and the world was cracked and scratched through the thick plastic windows. The floor was a sea of cigarette ends and dark patches of old chewing gum.

'At least the time break is getting so established that we should be able to find the exact moment it started,' Anna said, tapping her watch. 'We can find the precise moment that time stepped off the cliff.'

'Is that what you meant about finding the trigger?' I asked. 'You mean that we need to trace it right back to the root cause. To whatever went wrong, whenever it was, right at the start. The first step off the proper path.'

She nodded.

'Could be a long job.'

Anna stood up too. 'Come on, then. If you've finished sulking.'

'I wasn't sulking,' I protested.

'Not half.'

'I wasn't!'

'Look.' She turned round and glared at me. Just at that moment the street lights flickered into life as the evening closed in. Her face was suddenly bathed in an orange glow. Perhaps it was coincidence, or perhaps she'd timed it perfectly. Whichever, it was dramatic. It got my attention. 'Look – I need your help. And I need you at your best. Thinking, aware, on the case. You've had a couple of hours to get used to what's going on, to come to terms with the fact that everything's changed and you're a different person now. That's it. Time's up. Get with it.'

'Shape up or ship out,' I countered. Like Mr Pearson says in PE.

'Yes.'

'OK.'

'Good.' She thumped me lightly on the shoulder. It was a strangely friendly gesture, performed with a sad smile. 'Come on, then. Let's get a bit closer.'

We walked up the road and, standing under the trees that overhung the road from an adjacent garden, we played with time.

I hadn't a clue how to use my watch-thing, so Anna did the work. I just tried to see what she was up to, and remember. My watch was synchronized to hers, so it did whatever she did – and I went whenever she went.

'The defining moment, the trigger, is in the near future,' Anna said. 'Within the next day. The moment when a tiny little break in time finally opens up. From then it will grow and grow until . . .'

'I know, until the world falls into it. Or millions of people stop existing, or something equally terrible happens because time has gone off track.'

'You got it.'

Anna twisted the dial of her watch and the

world speeded up. It was night. Cars raced by so fast you could barely see them – a blistering thirty miles per hour, headlights streaking.

'How do we look to them?' I wondered.

'We don't look like anything. They can't see us.'

🕐 12TH OCTOBER (AGAIN)

The sun shot up into the sky like a rocket. Clouds whizzed past and an elderly lady with a walking stick sprinted by. The morning rush hour and school drop off were over in seconds.

'Getting there.' Anna was staring at the little read-out on her watch, the bit where mine showed the date.

The schoolkids got a second or two for lunch break.

'I'll slow it down a bit.'

We had a good view of the point where the hole in time would appear. We watched from further down the road – watched as time slowed to its normal pace.

'Any moment now.' Anna looked up from

her watch. 'I wonder what the trigger will—' She stopped abruptly.

So abruptly, her mouth just hanging open, that I wondered if time had stopped again and caught her. But her face quickly reshaped into a frown, her brow wrinkling before her eyes widened in horror.

'It can't be . . .' she murmured.

I looked round, to see where she was looking – staring at the point on the pavement where we knew the time break would later be. And there, standing at exactly that point, were Anna and I.

Both our watches chimed together. This was the moment.

Further along the pavement, my rucksack slipped off my shoulder. Just like I remembered.

Except . . .

Except this time, I could see the small imp-like creature with its stone-coloured leathery skin and wicked grin. Its claw-like hands had pulled the strap over my shoulder so that the rucksack fell.

'A Skitter,' Anna said. Her voice was flat and empty of either emotion or surprise. Numb. Like I felt. 'One of Midnight's.'

The Skitter was reaching inside the fallen rucksack, pulling out books and papers and folders, scattering them across the pavement. It took the history book, the one I had got that day, the one with the picture of the group of children from 1905 on the cover.

Anna – now-Anna – clutched at my arm. 'Oh, no,' I heard her murmur.

The devilish thing dropped the book, face up, on top of the others. Right where we were certain to see it, at then-Anna's feet. She couldn't miss it.

'That's the trigger?' I asked.

Anna nodded.

'I don't understand. How can chucking my books around change time, create some time problem or whatever?'

'That isn't what did it.' Her voice was small and quiet, almost embarrassed. Trembling. 'That's the cause, but the actual trigger was something else. Something that happened as a result of this moment.'

'But nothing happened,' I protested. 'Look.' I pointed at myself and Anna gathering up the books. 'We picked up my books. I put them away. I went home. End of story. That doesn't affect anything – how could it?'

'*You* went home,' now-Anna agreed.

We were watching the then me do it. But the then Anna ran off in the opposite direction. We watched her fiddling with the watch on her wrist and slowly fading from existence.

'*I* went back to 1905 and changed the photo. I thought I was being so clever. I thought it would prove things to you – convince you I was telling the truth. Instead . . .' I looked back at her and found Anna was staring intently at me. Her startling green eyes were welling up with tears. 'Don't you *see*? That's the trigger! That's what did it. I changed something I shouldn't have when I stood in front of the camera. History was changed – by me.'

'And that's it?' Something she had told me earlier was at the edge of my mind. 'But that means . . .'

'Oh, Jamie – I'm so sorry.'

'If you've already changed events, then you can't change them again because you're already part of them.' Was that what was upsetting her so much? 'You can't fix this because you're a part of it already. You caused it. Because of Midnight. Because of what he said, and what I told you about postcards from the past.'

'I was trying to save you, like you wanted me to,' she said. A tear ran down one of her cheeks. She made no effort to wipe it away. 'But I just made it worse. I did it, don't you see? You are lost because you fell into the time break. And I created the time break. All this – everything that's happened to you – is *my* fault.'

🕐 5TH MARCH 1941

How could Anna being in a picture suddenly change history? I didn't follow that at all, and I don't think she did either. She suggested that we go somewhere she knew, where we could get some peace and quiet to talk.

I imagined she meant a park bench or a café or something. I still wasn't used to the fact she – and I – could use history like other people use geography. It turned out that it wasn't some*where* we could go. It was some*when*.

It wasn't my idea of peace and quiet either. We sat in small, upright armchairs, the only light coming from a standard lamp that stood in the corner of the little room and a flickering candle on a low table. It was nicely kept – clean and uncluttered. But it seemed sort of grey and dull. No toys, no books, everything tidied away. Heavy curtains were pulled across the windows, but, even so, I could hear the explosions and the planes and the bell of an old-fashioned fire engine.

'I'm running out of air raids,' Anna confessed. 'I can't go back to one I've already used. But at least we can be sure the house is empty.'

'What if it gets hit by a bomb?' I asked rather nervously. As if to emphasise the point, there was an explosion close by. We felt the foundations of the house shake, followed by the sound of a plate or something smashing in the kitchen. The light went out and we were left sitting in near-darkness. 'Loads of London got blown up in the Blitz.'

'Including this bit. The house takes a direct hit and burns to the ground on 11th December 1941,' Anna said. She sounded like she was reading a card on an exhibit in a museum. 'Today's 5th March, so we're quite safe.'

'Yeah, well, what if we aren't?' I asked.

'We are.'

'And why do you want to come here, anyway? Why here and not, I dunno, midnight on the pier at Brighton in 1966 or something?'

'I was born here,' she said quietly. 'This is where I lived, just for a few months. Mum and Dad never talked about it, never mentioned losing everything they owned except for me. And now I've gone too. They've got nothing left.'

It was unusual for Anna to talk about herself. Unusual and refreshing. It made me feel like I wasn't the only one and that she really did understand. Not that she told me much. I guess not-being isn't much to tell.

'Dad was something in the civil service. During the war his job was protected — that means he wasn't called up to serve in the army or the navy or the air force. I don't know what he did, but I think it was quite important. After the war it was difficult, though. People didn't seem to understand why he hadn't fought. He was fighting in his own way, on the home front, he used to

111

say. It didn't bother him, or didn't seem to. But Mum got a lot of hassle for it.'

'Doesn't seem fair,' I said.

'It wasn't fair,' Anna snapped back. 'I like to think that Dad did more than anyone. I used to say that one day I'd go and see what he was really doing. Maybe he was a spy or a secret agent, or deciphering enemy codes or something.'

'Why don't you?' I asked. 'Go and find out, I mean.'

She shrugged. 'Never got round to it.' She changed the subject then, and I guessed the real reason was that she was scared of what she'd find out about her dad. Maybe he'd been an office clerk, or in charge of egg production in Lincolnshire, or taking messages for some government minister. Something trivial and boring.

'They didn't have much, Mum and Dad. But they had a child that they loved very much.' She stared away into the distance, avoiding looking at me as the bombs dropped outside. 'And then, one day, they didn't even have her. Just gone. And you know the worst thing?'

'Yes,' I said quietly.

'The worst thing is that they never even knew they had a daughter.'

'I know.'

'Time does that. It plays games, it messes you up.' She lapsed into silence.

Eventually, I summoned enough courage to break into her lonely thoughts. 'How can the time break thing have happened then? With the photo?'

'I don't know. I've been wondering that. Either someone there when the picture was taken was affected by seeing me, or . . .' She paused as more fire engines went past. Someone was shouting near by, calling for water. And the bombs kept on falling.

'Or what?'

'Or someone saw me in the photo after it was taken. Maybe years after.'

'Then we need to know the history of the photograph,' I said, thinking out loud. 'Like where it appears, where it's printed. Can't just be that one book, can it? It'll be in a library or a shop or on the internet or something.'

'And someone somewhen saw it and as a result

they did something that changed everything.' She stood up and wandered round the room. There was a familiarity in her movement – as if she really was at home here.

'Is it really that simple?' I asked. 'I mean, if so why isn't history changed every time you and other Runners go into action?' I wondered how often she had returned, how many air raids, how many hours, she had spent here alone. She could never come back to the same night or she'd meet herself, so there was a limit to the number of times she could come. Had she nearly used them all up?

'History *is* changed by us – it changes all the time. But tiny, little changes, like ripples in a pond. This one – it's like someone chucked in a huge boulder.'

'Big change, then.'

'Not just big. It's created some problem or conflict that time can't sort out. It's not like ...' She paused, trying to decide what it wasn't like. 'It's not like you miss a train and that changes history. You just catch the next one, and maybe you do the same things a few hours later until you catch up with yourself. Time sorts itself out. But in this case . . .' She waved her hands in frustration.

The constant drone of the aircraft high above us seemed to be diminishing now. 'I think I see,' I told her. 'It's like you miss the train, but then that train crashes and you would have been in hospital for months, or dead even, and now you're not. So it's all different. *Very* different. Is that it?'

'Sort of,' she agreed.

'But our time break is more than that, isn't it? So what we're looking for is big. A mega change. Huge.'

'Yes.'

'Where do we start?' I asked.

'1905. When the picture was taken. It's the one date and place we do know.' She held out her hand. 'The all clear will sound in a few minutes and the people who live here will be back. With their baby. With *me*. Come on.'

🕐 17th May 1905

I didn't ask where we were going because, I guess, I was already beginning to see time as more important than place.

We arrived in an alleyway between the backs of two rows of narrow town houses. I could hear women laughing and children playing. It didn't look like the alleyway was used much – the paving was overgrown with weeds and grass, and there was litter scattered along it – pages of newspaper, broken bottles, an old wooden crate that was rotting to pieces . . .

The alleyway emerged on to the pavement beside a narrow road. Actually it was little more than a track, though there were grey town houses along both sides. Anna led the way down the street. She knew where she was going, of course – she'd been here before, when she got into the picture.

A horse clattered past, pulling a long, low cart. The cart was loaded with old-fashioned milk churns. The driver sat looking bored and tired on a bench across the front of the cart. He and the horse both ignored us. Just kids. We were wearing long nondescript coats, so we didn't stand out. Obviously.

The road met another, which widened almost immediately into a sort of town square. On one side was a church, crushed in between yet more houses. On the other, opposite the church, was a school. It looked very much like the older bits of my own primary school – a long, tall building with a steep tiled roof. A stone wall separated the school and its playground from the road outside.

As we watched, a group of children emerged from a gate, laughing and talking. A man in a severe, dark suit ushered them along to the pavement outside the wall. Another man was carrying a wooden tripod with a large camera mounted on it. It was obviously heavy. He splayed out the legs and set up the camera in the street – making me realise that I had seen no traffic apart from the horse and cart.

The children, perhaps a dozen of them, were crowding round in front of the wall, being vaguely organised by the man in the suit. The photographer had disappeared under a long black drape which hung over the back of the camera.

Happy at last, the man in the suit walked over to join the photographer. As soon as he left them, the boys and girls started jostling for position and shoving each other around again. Some things don't change much, I thought. A boy wearing a jacket that was far too small for him pushed his way to the front and stood next to short dark-haired girl. She glanced at him nervously. I saw she was holding a cloth doll which she clutched tightly.

'Everyone, still please!' came a muffled shout from beneath the canopy.

'This is it,' Anna said.

We were watching from across the street. No one seemed to have noticed us at all.

'All looks perfectly normal so far,' I said to Anna. 'Here you come.'

I had seen her head bob up for a moment above the stone school wall, by the gate. She was timing her entrance. Now, as the children calmed down and settled into their pose, Anna – the then Anna who had come here to prove to me she could travel in time – ran from the school gate and barged her way quickly in front of the camera.

She wriggled into position beside the boy with the small jacket, shoving the dark-haired girl back. It was like Anna had shoved me too. I felt it then – a punch to the stomach that made me feel suddenly sick, just for a second. That was it, I knew – like when Midnight was coming, I could feel it. The moment.

I heard a cry of surprise and saw the doll fall to the ground behind Anna. A tiny hand reached down for it, the rest of the figure hidden from my view and the camera's.

Then it was over. The photographer emerged from under the canopy. The man in the suit strode over, perhaps to tell Anna off. But she wasn't there. She had pushed her way back through the children, out of sight, by the wall. And when they all moved aside, she was gone.

'They'll explain it away.' Anna shifted un-comfortably from foot to foot, anxious to move away in case she was spotted. 'They'll decide I wasn't there at all, or that I was another girl from the school, or visiting or something.'

'What if they don't, though?' I said. 'What if *that's* the difference? What if seeing a ghost is what's affected someone here so much it changes history?'

'They've forgotten me already. And when they see the picture they'll find an explanation.'

Certainly the children and the two men seemed to be heading back into the school quite happily. The children were talking loudly, pushing and shoving each other through the gate. The man was shouting at them to pipe down, and the photographer was keeping well back to avoid getting his camera knocked about.

In a minute the place was empty and quiet once more.

'That was the moment,' I said. 'I felt it.'

'There must be something,' Anna said. 'Something new. Something's in that picture that shouldn't be there. It can't be just me. I'm already lost, I won't make waves. It can't be me.' She sounded like she was trying to convince herself more than anyone else.

But I was already thinking along different lines. What if she was wrong?

What if it *wasn't* something that had been added to the picture?

'We need to trace the history of the photograph,' Anna was saying. 'We might be able to work out what's been added.'

'Or removed,' I said suddenly.

She turned to look at me, like she'd forgotten I was even there.

'What if it isn't something new in the picture?' I said. 'What if it's something that should be there, but which is now missing?'

'Like what?'

I shrugged. 'Like a little girl with a doll.'

🕐 AT THE END OF TIME

It was a vast, circular room filled with books. The bookcases were curved so they echoed the shape of the walls which I could just about make out in the distance. At intervals, spiral staircases snaked upwards to the next level. And the next and the next. Looking up, the structure seemed to disappear into infinity. It made me feel quite dizzy – like in a big old church, when you crane your head back to see the roof so high above.

Maybe there *was* no roof. All I could see was a succession of circular walkways extending for ever. And in the middle of the huge floor on which we stood was a circular hole. Even before

I reached the polished wooden railing that ran round the edge of it, I knew what I would see when I looked down. Sure enough, the floors below disappeared into oblivion and darkness. I leaned out as far as I dared, hoping to see more. The floors I could see looked identical to the one we were on.

Senex was sitting at a table positioned between the curved bookcases, examining a book. It was a round table, of course. Everything was round or curved, feeding back on itself. It all went on for ever – twisting and curling through all eternity.

'Where are we?' I asked Anna as she joined me at the rail.

'The Library at the End of Time,' she said, as if this was the most obvious and the most ordinary thing in the whole world. 'It's the place to discover the history of that photograph and everyone in it, or *not* in it.'

Anna led me past several bookcases to where Senex was sitting. All the books seemed identical – bound in dark leather and dusty, untitled. That included the volumes on the table and the one that the old man was examining. I could see as I

123

got closer that the pages were not paper, but were more like the stuff they make the screens of laptop computers out of. But they weren't that either.

I watched Senex as he examined page after page of the curious material. I saw information scroll past, pictures come and go, people moving across the book . . .

'You were careless,' Senex said after several minutes. He looked sternly at Anna. 'To say the least.'

She shuffled her feet in embarrassment. 'I'm sorry,' she murmured.

'It wasn't her fault,' I said, surprised Anna wasn't sticking up for herself. 'Midnight . . .'

'Tricked her,' Senex interrupted. 'Through you, he got to Anna. I know. Which is why I am not as angry as perhaps I should be.' He stared off into the distance, into the depths of his own memories. 'Midnight, in his time, has tricked us all.' He sighed. 'So there is no point in anger, or punishment. But at least we have a clearer idea of some of what happened now.'

'That was quick.' I was impressed. He must

have known where to look. 'We only just got here.'

The man looked up at me with something close to pity. 'You might have only just arrived, but I've been here for many hours.' Then he smiled, as if remembering I was new to all this and needed to be humoured. He stood up and stretched his arms out expansively, to encompass the whole vast place. 'As Anna has no doubt already told you, this is the Library at the End of Time,' he announced. 'Here is stored all the information, all the history, all the knowledge.'

'About what?'

'About everything,' Anna told me.

'Why "at the end of time", though?'

'Because if the library existed any sooner, it couldn't be complete, could it?' Anna retorted. 'There'd be stuff that hadn't been discovered yet. History that hadn't happened. People who hadn't yet lived to have their biographies written and their lives catalogued.'

'The library contains *everything*,' Senex said. 'All of history from the absolute beginning to the very end of time. Not just history that happened, but history that might have happened. Oh, yes,' he said with a smile, 'you are in here too. Even though you are lost, your story is here – a might-have-been history.'

I whistled. 'That's a lot of history.'

'I thought you found history boring,' Anna retorted.

I nodded. 'I quite like books, though.' I was thinking about what they had told me. 'So if might-have-been history is here as well, then we just have to work out the difference between what should have happened and what did happen. Or whatever.'

'Is that all?' Anna said. She was still sulking a little from Senex's rebuke, even though he'd made a point of not telling her off. Sometimes that's worse, of course.

Senex was more patient with me. 'The difficulty is that there are so many possible differences. There are possible histories where – for whatever reason – the photo was never taken at all. There are others where perhaps the whole process of photography was never invented. It is not as simple as you make it sound. We must draw our comparisons carefully and we must be sure of why the differences occur. We must trace back the right difference, to the right cause. Matching up cause and effect is not always easy, you know.'

'But you've done it before, haven't you?' I said. 'You can show us what to do – how to get started.'

Senex smiled. 'Very well.' He opened one of the books and gestured for Anna and me to sit beside him so that we could see. 'I would suggest you start with the lives of everyone in that photograph. Trace each and every one through time – see who they met and what they did. Somewhere, somewhen, there will be a connection that should not have been made, or a connection that should be there but is broken. When you find that, you have found the problem . . .'

Henry Masterson was something of a recluse in his old age. He outlived his wife and had no surviving children. But what he *did* have was a vast fortune. He was no longer involved in the day-to-day running of the company he founded

127

in 1855, which pioneered the use of a new kind of power loom to weave cloth. It was cheaper and more efficient than the competition, and the company flourished.

So in his later years, Masterson was able to leave the running of the company to others while he lived alone in his huge house on the outskirts of London. Just him and his memories.

The most painful of these memories was the day his daughter died. Mary-Ann was eleven years' old when she caught the flu. She battled against it for almost a week before finally giving up the struggle. She was buried in the local church, on the village square, opposite the school.

Masterson's wife never recovered from her grief at the loss of their daughter. She herself passed away ten years later, but inside she was dead already. Outwardly, Masterson seemed to recover from both losses well. He threw himself fiercely into the business and took the firm to greater heights, making even larger profits.

But by the start of the new century he was tired and lonely and bitter. He had all the money, all the wealth he could possibly want. But no one to spend it on, no one to leave it to, no one to care for.

Until he met Jane Sinclair.

She was a local girl, eleven years' old. He spotted her quite by chance one day in the local paper, and immediately he could see that she was the image of his own daughter. Her age, her height, her hair, the way she smiled nervously – they all seemed so familiar. Perhaps it was just wishful thinking on his part, perhaps his memories of Mary-Ann were distorted by the thirty years since she had died. Masterson was no fool, he did not for one moment believe that his daughter had returned, somehow reincarnated. But he wanted to meet the girl anyway, to get to know her, to furnish her with just a little of the love he would have given his daughter.

The Sinclair family thought it a little odd, but they did not stop Jane from visiting the old man in the big house. They didn't know who he really was, just that he never went out and rarely had visitors. And if he sent Jane home with a gift of an antique clock or a roll of the most exquisite machine-woven cloth, then that was all to the good. The family struggled to get by on Mr Sinclair's wages and Jane's mother was forced to take in laundry, which she hated. She hated the laundry, and she hated the fact that she had to do it.

As Jane grew older, her attachment to the old man became more pronounced. She saw him as the grandfather she had never known. And as he grew old and weak and infirm, he came to rely on her to look after him as well as for company. When she should have left school, he made sure she got into the local grammar school and he paid the fees.

Jane was inconsolable when the old man died. It was 1909 and she was fifteen years' old. The money that Masterson left in trust for her paid for the rest of her education, and Jane's mother stopped taking in laundry. When Jane was twenty-one she inherited Masterson's fortune – his house, his money, his business.

Jane Sinclair was a shrewd and clever woman by now, and she could see that woven cloth was not the way of the future. When the Great War came in 1914, she secured a government grant to switch some of the company's manufacturing to engineering components for artillery and – later – the new tanks that would soon dominate the battlefields in Europe.

By the time the Second World War started in 1939, the company was making aircraft parts as well. It designed and manufactured a vital engine sub-assembly for the new Spitfire – the plane that, together with the Hurricane, won the Battle of Britain and drove off the threat of a Nazi invasion.

'Except,' Anna told Senex, 'it never happened.' She closed the book.

'Masterson left the company to some distant cousin, who just wanted to make as much money out of it as possible,' I explained. 'It carried on making and selling cloth, but the quality went right down and pretty soon the orders were going down too. The guy had no idea about business.'

Senex stood up and walked slowly round the table. He looked down at the page in the book in front of Anna and me. 'By the mid-1920s the company had gone bankrupt,' he said. 'Yes, I think you have found it.'

'There's more,' Anna told him.

Indeed there was. We'd been busy. I had thought it would be like homework – boring and dull. But when everything you read about is suddenly real and has an effect, that gives it an edge. I was surprised that I had actually enjoyed going through the books with Anna and working out the puzzle of how history had changed. How that tiny event – someone just standing in a photograph – had made such a difference.

Senex was standing on the other side of the table now. He leaned across, hands flat on the table top as he listened to Anna.

'It meant that the Spitfire's engine was nothing like as efficient and impressive as it should have been,' she said. 'The plane was hardly a match for the German Messerschmitt fighters in the Battle of Britain. In the summer of 1940, the German army landed on the south coast in force. An invasion.'

She broke off at that point, and I remembered sitting in the house with her during the Blitz. It was all much closer to her home, her time, than to mine. But even so, I was affected by it too. With Senex's help, we pieced together the rest of the story – the rest of what history might have become . . .

'Time has a way of sorting these things out,' Senex told us, opening another book and gesturing for us to look. I wondered if he had known all along what we would find, or if he was just used to following the threads of history through time. 'With the early intervention of America,' he explained, 'the allied forces regrouped and drove the German armies back into Europe. It took a little longer, but by 1948 Berlin had fallen and the war was over.'

Together with Senex, Anna and I read the remaining documents and accounts in the books. My grandfather had been killed in the invasion. I read his name in the list of the dead in a newspaper clipping that appeared on one of the pages in one of the books. I didn't need him to tell me what that meant. Grandad had died before he was married. So my father was never born, and neither was I.

'The effects of the change are rippling forwards,' Senex told us. 'Just as the effects of the time break are rippling backwards. Reality must be put back on track.'

'And if it isn't?' I asked.

'Then it won't just be you who is lost,' Anna said. 'It'll be your grandad, and your father, and your sister.'

'And countless other casualties,' Senex added.

But I hardly heard him. 'Ellie,' I murmured. And I realised, maybe for the first time, how much I missed her. 'And all because of a picture,' I said bitterly. 'All because Masterson never saw Jane Sinclair in a picture in the paper.'

Anna said nothing. She turned away from us, her shoulders trembling as she stared out over the gaping hole in the centre of the Library.

'So Masterson never saw her picture in the local newspaper,' Senex said quietly. 'He was never struck by how much she looked like his own daughter. Never arranged to meet her. They never became friends and he never left her anything . . .' He sighed loudly. 'The rest, as they say, is history.'

'No,' I said loudly, angrily. 'No, it isn't, not yet. We can change it back. We can fix it. We have to.'

'Can we?' Anna spoke without turning round. Her voice was strained and quiet.

I went over and put my hands on her shoulders. It felt a bit weird, because she's slightly taller than me, so I had to reach up. 'Yes, we can,' I told her firmly. 'We can't change what you did, but we can alter other things. We can still get history back on track. I've got an idea. But I need your help.'

Senex shook our hands solemnly. 'You'll be all right, you know, young man.'

'Thanks.' I meant it. His confidence in our ability to sort this out was encouraging, even though I wasn't nearly as sure about my idea as I was making out.

So we were on our own again – just Anna and me. Senex had another assignment and was needed to deal with a Skitter that was causing trouble in medieval Russia.

'It's got the local farmers watching television and installed a pinball machine at the local inn,' Senex told us seriously. 'I can only assume it thinks that no one will notice pockets of the twenty-first century appearing a few hundred years early.'

'They just like causing trouble,' Anna said. She seemed to have recovered some of her humour, but I could tell she was still blaming herself.

'Midnight manipulated us both,' I said. 'He put the words into my mouth, his Skitter made sure you saw that picture and got the idea . . .'

'But I still fell for it. I should have known better.'

'You'll know next time.'

'There won't be a next time.'

'There you go then.' I grinned, though I wasn't actually feeling that great about things. But it seemed to cheer her up.

She reached for her watch. 'Back to 1905, I guess.'

'Midnight will be expecting that,' I said. 'Let's make it 1907. Doesn't matter exactly when. So long as it's before 1909, when Masterson dies.'

'I suppose.'

'Show me how to set my watch,' I said. 'I'll meet you there.'

She smiled. 'Want to prove you can manage on your own?'

'I might have to,' I pointed out. 'But actually, I want to go somewhere else first. Some*when* else, I should say.' I told her which point in time I wanted to visit.

Anna wasn't keen. 'But why? We have to get moving.'

'Oh?'

'No, really, we do. The time break won't wait for us. Its effects are growing all the while, it doesn't matter where or when we are. The longer we leave it, the worse it gets. It's spreading through time, growing, causing havoc. And it's sucking in everything along the way that shouldn't be there in the new version of history.'

'Including my family,' I reminded her. 'If we don't put things right, then it won't just be me who's lost. But I still want to go.'

'Why? It's happened, gone, past. Just leave it.'

I didn't want to argue, but I didn't want to tell her why either. 'Look,' I said as calmly as I could, 'you have the house in the Blitz, where you were born. You want to keep going back there. I just want to go back to my school, that's all.'

'You didn't even like it there.'

'That's not the point. Just show me how, and I'll meet you in 1907. You won't even know I've been.' If I didn't need her help to get there, I wouldn't have mentioned it. I think she realised that.

She showed me what to do, but I could tell she wasn't happy. It was all very terse and abrupt. Do this, do that, twist here . . .

'I'll see you soon,' I said. 'I'll only be a second.'

She smiled at that. Then we were both gone.

🕐 12TH OCTOBER (THIRD TIME LUCKY!)

No one took much notice of me. Another kid wandering round the school between lessons. I reckoned I had the hang of the watch thing now, or at least enough for what I wanted to do.

It was just after break and the *then me* would have had History now. I headed over to the History classroom. There was a window in the door, so I knew I'd be able to see into the room. I just wanted to see myself, in some semblance of normality. Sitting in class that last day.

It was interesting to watch. I don't just mean seeing myself, like in pictures or on video or something. Though looking through the small oblong window it seemed like the class was happening on a screen rather than in real life. No, I mean the way everyone behaved as if I wasn't there with them in the room.

Since I could see myself, maybe it was more obvious watching it as an observer than it had been when I was in the middle of it. The centre of unattention. The thin black wires running diagonally through the glass to strengthen it made it look as if I'd been crossed out. It was most noticeable when Mike Ibbotson handed out the books. He walked between the rows of desks, giving a book to everyone. I counted as he took each book off the top of his pile. And of course when he got to me, he just went on to the next desk without offering a book.

I almost laughed out loud at the look on my face, but inside I was so sad. There I was, hand out ready to take a book, and the boy just walked right past without even a glance. I looked round, and saw nothing – not even myself at the window. Then I got angry and shouted. Mike turned, though I wasn't sure if he had really heard, or if he really saw me even then. I stood up and grabbed a book off the top of the pile. He shrugged, as if he'd been distracted by something outside, and went on handing out books.

Half an hour earlier, in the break *before* the lesson, the classroom was empty. I stood alone in the room, by Mr Postlethwaite's desk – a quick and easy backward wind of the watch. Soon I would come in and Ibbotson would not hand me a book. Again, but also for the first time. And I'd be watching myself as it happened. Anna was right – time was a confusing web of criss-crossing paths rather than a single straight line.

There were several piles of history books at the side of the desk, ready to be given out to different classes. All similar. Different titles in the same series. Would Anna be on the cover of the book for our class? After all, the photo had been taken with her in it. Or would the book show the photo before she was in it, as it should have been? I hardly dared look.

But I did. And Anna was there, grinning back at me, with no idea what she had just done. History was changing. It had already changed to this point, and I needed to hurry if we were to change it back. I ran my finger down the pile of books, feeling it bump over the edges of the spines. Time to sort things out, I decided. Because I knew what I could do. It had just been a vague thought, the start of an idea when I insisted to Anna that I should come here. Now I knew what I *had* to do . . .

🕐 2ND FEBRUARY 1907

It was a cold winter's day and there was a sprinkling of snow on the ground. I could tell from the few footprints that Anna had not been waiting long.

'You all right?' she asked.

I nodded. 'Just needed to get some things sorted out.'

'I know.' She kicked the spattering of snow off

the toes of her shoes. 'Look, I'm sorry I was annoyed with you.'

'It's OK.'

I guessed she was nervous and blaming herself still. 'Thanks.'

The Sinclair family, including Jane, who would now be thirteen, lived in a narrow town house squashed between two other narrow town houses in a whole road of narrow town houses. It was just round the corner from the school and the church. The school where Jane went, and the church where Masterson's daughter was buried.

'Should be easy enough,' I said.

'Should be.' Anna raised her eyebrows, checking it was OK. When I nodded, she turned and knocked on the door.

We had talked it through with Senex in the library and he had assured us that the plan was sound. Since Anna was already in the picture, since she had already changed things we couldn't change back – like we couldn't go and pull poor Jane Sinclair back in front of Anna, or intercept Anna on her dash from the school gate – we had to find another way to achieve the same result as the picture.

The easiest thing was simply to take Jane and introduce her to Masterson, then let events take their course. When he met Jane, the old man would see the similarity to his daughter, just as he had in the photo when it was in the paper. Time would pick up the loose ends and knit them together and everything would snap back into place. Obvious, really.

Except that what we were planning was *so* obvious that Midnight was sure to have thought of it. Whatever his reason for wanting to mess about with time and change things round, whatever he thought he could achieve, he would try and stop us. That's what he does.

So we came to 1907 instead of 1905 – hoping he wouldn't expect that. Hoping he wouldn't be able to trace us.

'I'll get it, Mum,' came a call from inside. A girl's voice.

I winked at Anna. She gave me a 'don't get cocky, we're not there yet' look in return. Then we both turned to see who was opening the door.

It was a girl of about my age. Two years can change you a lot, but I wouldn't have guessed she was the girl clutching the doll. She looked taller, with her hair cut a bit shorter, wearing different clothes obviously. She was changed out of all recognition.

'Yeah?' she said. 'You after Mum? I can get her for you. Whose washing is it you're after?'

'Sorry?' I was struggling already.

'You've come for the laundry.' It wasn't a question. Maybe that was the only reason anyone called – to drop off or collect the laundry. But she could see we weren't dropping laundry off. Not unless we were about to undress in the street and hand over the clothes we were standing there in. Unlikely. Especially in the snow.

'Actually, we came to see you, Jane,' Anna said. She seemed to have more of a handle on things than I did just then.

'Me?'

'You *are* Jane Sinclair?' I asked. After all, we didn't want to get the wrong girl.

'That's me. Who wants to know?' She was wary now, her eyes narrowed and suspicious.

'It's all right,' Anna assured her. 'We want to help. We need to talk to you for a minute, that's all.'

'So, talk.' She folded her arms, challenging us to make it interesting and worth her while.

'I'm Jamie,' I said. 'This is Anna.'

Jane nodded, as much as to say, 'And?'

'There's . . .' Anna paused, deciding what to say. 'There's someone we'd like you to meet,' she said at last.

I nodded, hoping that would help.

'Oh? Who?' She wasn't convinced. 'Why?'

'It's for your own good,' I said quickly.

She nodded again, as if that made sense. 'S'what they say at school when they beat you.'

OK, so maybe that wasn't the best choice of words. I tried again. 'No, really. He wants to meet you. I think you'll be friends.'

'You saying I've got no mates?'

This wasn't going too well. But at least she was here and was listening. So far. I looked at Anna – her turn.

'Have you heard of Henry Masterson?' Anna said.

146

'You're kidding, right?'

'No, I'm not kidding.'

'He wants to see you,' I put in.

'What, now?'

'Soon as you can,' I replied.

'Why didn't you say?' She sighed, turned and went back inside.

'Oh, well done,' Anna hissed. 'Now you've scared her off.'

'Have I?' I wasn't so sure. She hadn't closed the door, and from her reaction to Masterson's name I was beginning to hope that—

My hopes were cut short by Jane's reappearance. She was struggling into a threadbare coat. She called out over her shoulder as she stepped out to join us, 'Just going out, Mum. Some people have come for me, I won't be long.' She pulled the door shut without waiting for an answer. 'So what's Mr Masterson want?'

She seemed to know the way – which was more than we did. Yes, we'd looked at a map from the period in the library, but translating that into the actual landscape was not as easy as it sounded. So we let Jane lead the way.

'I guess he's something of a local celebrity,' Anna said quietly to me. 'Even though he doesn't go out much.'

'He's been here a long time,' I agreed. 'Probably the fact no one ever sees him adds to the mystique.'

'The what?'

'Makes him seem even more interesting.'

'Oh. Right.'

Jane had paused ahead of us. She turned to shout, 'You coming too?' Then carried on.

We hurried to catch up. All the time I was looking round, keeping an eye out for Midnight or one of his creatures. Would I feel him in the pit of my stomach like before? Or would he just appear to stop us and laugh in our faces, to deride our ridiculous plan?

But we reached the rusty iron gates that barred the overgrown driveway leading up to the dilapidated old house where Masterson lived without any sign of Midnight. I was beginning to think we might get away with it. The oil-less creak of the opening gate drove thoughts of Midnight from my head and we started up the drive.

It was cobbled, with weeds and grass poking between the stones where the mortar or cement or tar or whatever it was had aged and crumbled. The house looked like it had been wrapped in ivy to hold it together and I felt a bit like Prince Charming happening across Sleeping Beauty's castle a hundred years after everyone else had forgotten it even existed.

'So why's he want to see me?' Jane said. She was walking slowly, perhaps nervous of meeting the local legend.

'I don't know,' Anna said, glancing at me. 'But it seemed to be urgent.'

'I think maybe you remind him of someone,' I added, hoping that was vague enough while perhaps also sowing an idea in her mind. She seemed very calm, almost resigned about meeting Masterson. I guessed that was good.

But Jane was looking at me like I was daft. 'You've never even met him, have you?' she said.

Were we being that obvious? I expected her to turn and run off, realising she was being tricked in some way. But instead she shook her head in amused disbelief and carried on up the drive.

'He does want to see you,' Anna said firmly.

'Course he does.' She didn't look back. Again we hurried after her.

'She's gained a bit of confidence in the last two years, hasn't she?' I said to Anna.

'What do you mean?'

'I mean she wouldn't let you push her aside and trample her dolly now.'

Anna just glared.

'Joke,' I explained. 'Ha ha.'

She wasn't impressed.

Ahead of us, Jane was waiting at the front door.

'Moment of truth,' Anna murmured, and we hurried to join her.

Anna reached for the thin iron rod that was the bell pull. It was flaking with rust.

'That doesn't work,' Jane said, though I hadn't seen her try it. 'Anyway,' she went on, pushing the door open, 'it's not locked.'

'We can't just—' Anna began.

'Yes, we can,' I told her, and pushed the door fully open. It protested and creaked and scraped over the tiled floor of the entrance hall.

I thought at first that the ivy had got inside

and was growing across the floor and up the walls and the dusty staircase that swept away in front of us. But it was the sunlight shining through the ivy-clad windows. The shadows of the real creepers and branches outside clung darkly to the inside of the house. The whole place could have been deserted and abandoned were it not for the trail of footprints crossing and re-crossing the dusty floor and up and down the bare wooden boards of the staircase.

That and the voice.

'In the study,' it called. It was an old, slightly cracked voice – as dusty as the owner's house. 'Come on through. Oh, and close the door behind you, would you please?'

Anna pushed the door shut, and I followed Jane past the staircase. She seemed to know where the voice had come from and led the way. She went to an oak-panelled door opposite and behind the stairs. It was standing ajar and she pushed it open, stepped into the room, and froze.

I followed her in, Anna catching up with us as we stepped inside. Jane remained on the threshold, staring into the study, immobile.

A second later, Anna and I also stopped dead in our tracks.

It was a large room, with dark wooden panelling all round. Shutters were closed across the windows, one section left open to allow patches of weak, dusty sunlight to shine in past the grime and the ivy that coated the windows. They illuminated a desk piled with papers and journals, books and files.

There were two chairs in the room and both were facing away from the door. One was a large armchair, close to where we stood and positioned so that it faced the desk – a visitor's chair. The other was an upright wooden chair on the other side of the desk. A swivel chair that was facing away from us towards the bookcase, as if whoever was sitting in it had turned from the desk to find a particular book. Now it was swinging back round. We were about to meet Henry Masterson.

The chair turned slowly. The light cut across the desk and the chair in slices and fractions. So the true horror of the sight was only revealed in glimpses and moments. A suit that was falling apart as the threads and material crumbled to dust. Hands that were just bone clutching the shattered remains of a fountain pen. And the skull of a face – teeth rotting, blank eye sockets staring, bone flaking away. Aged almost beyond recognition.

'He's been dead for years,' I realised out loud.

And as if disturbed by the sound of my voice, the skeleton seemed to give a sigh and fell forwards across the desk. The skull split from the spine with a crack like my dad makes with his knuckles and rolled across the blotter. It fell to the floor, still staring at us, grinning at us, jaw crumbling so it sank lopsided into the dust and decay.

'But he called out,' Anna said. 'And he isn't supposed to be dead. Not yet. Not until 1909, not for another two years.'

We both looked to Jane, to see how she was coping with this horrific scene.

She hadn't moved.

Didn't move.

Frozen in time. I felt suddenly sick.

'I'm afraid there's been a slight change to the

schedule.' The voice came from the armchair. A voice we recognised as it changed from old and cracked to young and dark. It didn't seem much of a surprise – not after the sight of Masterson's body. I just stared in mute acceptance as Midnight got up from the chair.

'I knew you would get to Jane,' he said, waving his cane in front of her sightless eyes. 'But you need Masterson too, of course.' He was smiling horribly. Like the skull that was crumbling on the carpet. 'Only now you're too late. I got here a few minutes ahead of you, and so, as you can see . . .' He waved the cane in the direction of the desk, of the skeleton. 'The poor man has been dead for over a century.'

· CHAPTER ELEVEN ·

Midnight left Jane Sinclair frozen in position.
Two goblin-like figures sprang into view beside
him and escorted myself and Anna out of the
ivy-covered house. They leaped and jumped
and hopped like Year 2 kids on an outing. All
the time they were giggling – at least, I think they
were. Their stony faces were contorted into what
might be grins, and the sound was like chalk
breaking on an old blackboard coupled with a
machine gun going off at double speed.

'She will wake later and be none the wiser,'
Midnight assured us. 'She will go home, not
knowing why she came here, or where you went,
or what happened to a few hours of her life.

She'll always wonder, and never know.' He seemed to find this funny, and I guessed it was the only reason he'd let the poor girl go.

I didn't complain.

Nor did Anna. She was obviously scared of the goblin-like Skitters. They could sense it, and their talon-fingers raked within inches of her as they cackled away like old witches on fast forward.

'And anyway,' Midnight said, 'I wouldn't want her to miss all the fun.'

'What fun?' I asked glumly, trying myself to keep clear of the nasty creatures that were constantly circling us. They scared me too.

'The way the world collapses in on itself. The way history disintegrates. The way time tries to sort out and tie up its loose ends. And fails, sucking oh so many people into the abyss.' Midnight was smiling, as if I'd just invited him home for tea. 'It should be so much fun. I adore chaos and death, don't you?'

'What do you think?'

He considered this. 'I think,' he said after a few moments, 'that you should both come with me and see how it will all turn out.'

'Why don't you just let us go?' Anna said. She looked pale and her voice was strained. 'You've won, so go and gloat and leave us alone. Haven't you done enough? Can't you see you've won and everything will fall apart? Just leave us!'

Midnight seemed scandalized by the suggestion. 'Oh I couldn't possibly do that. I really do think you should see for yourselves the results of your ineptitude and stupidity.' He raised his hand and snapped his fingers.

And suddenly, we were gone.

🕐 13TH OCTOBER (YET AGAIN!)

I don't know what Midnight was expecting, but this certainly wasn't it. I could tell from his expression – the way the smile froze as if he'd been stopped in time like Jane Sinclair. Slowly, as if in disbelief, the smile faded in the bright sunlight.

Anna was looking at me. She'd seen Midnight's smile fade away, and she'd probably seen my own arrive. I tried to keep a straight face, but I could feel that it wasn't working. I didn't know, not

157

yet – but from Midnight's reaction I hoped that everything was going to sort itself out now.

'Problem?' I asked, trying to sound innocent.

'How did ...' Midnight turned a full circle. The Skitters had vanished again, though I could sense they were there. I could almost see the air moving round them as they too turned and spun and looked.

We were back outside school, on the pavement where the hole caused by the time break had been. Or rather would be. Or rather – I hoped – would never be. If Midnight had expected to find the rip through time waiting there, growing, sucking in everything from a changing world, then he was as disappointed as I was delighted.

His face was as dark as his name. He stepped slowly and very menacingly towards me and, despite myself, I stepped back. Surprisingly, Anna stepped between us, looking up defiantly at Midnight. Well, it surprised me.

'What have you done?' Midnight hissed. The words seemed to echo, as if the Skitters were saying it too, just a millisecond behind him.

'Nothing,' I said. 'And nor has Anna.'

He still didn't get it. And neither did she.

'And that's the problem, isn't it?' I went on. For the first time I was wondering how we'd get away. My hand was on my watch dial, but Midnight had stopped Anna's watch from working before when he was close to her – would he, could he do it again?

I said, 'The time break, everything, was caused by Anna going back and appearing in that picture. By her obscuring Jane Sinclair so she was never in the photo and Masterson never saw her.'

'Obviously.' He managed to sound bored and menacing at the same time. Maybe he was coming to the conclusion that I wasn't clever enough to have beaten him and there was some other explanation. In which case he would kill us as easily as he had Henry Masterson. So I had to keep him interested until we could escape.

Anna was watching me closely. Despite being as afraid of Midnight as I was, she was curious too.

'I killed Masterson before they could meet,' Midnight hissed. Again there was an unearthly echo to his words.

'It never happened,' I said simply. 'Anna was never in that picture.' Anna and I were standing side by side now. I reached out and took her hand, our bodies hiding this from Midnight. Not that I meant anything by it. Not that I had a plan or anything. I just wanted to know she was there with me, and I thought she'd feel the same.

'But I was,' she said quietly. 'I went back. He tricked me and I went back to get in the photo.'

'You killed Masterson in 1907,' I said to Midnight. 'I guess you just wanted the pleasure of being there to see us fail. Just wanted to show us how stupid we were and how clever you are. But you can't go back and change your mind now, you've already done it.'

He glared at us through coal-black eyes. He could see what I had done, and he was wondering *how* I'd done it. That curiosity was probably all that was keeping us alive. 'So?'

'So Masterson had *already* met Jane. She knew who he was, where he lived, the way to the house. Even where the study was.' I was getting more confident now. 'They already knew each other, and he'd already made his will – leaving everything to her.'

'When she was twenty-one,' Anna remembered. 'In trust, so that she gets the money at the same time no matter when Masterson dies. That doesn't change at all. But how did they meet?'

'He saw her picture in the paper,' Midnight said, staring at me accusingly. His voice was quiet – quiet as the grave. He'd worked it out, and that meant we were in big trouble.

But Anna still looked confused. I smiled, or tried to. But inside I was terrified. 'I swapped the book,' I said. 'I made sure I got the wrong book when they were handed out in history. I went back and put a different book in the pile. The photo you're in – it isn't the picture of Jane at all. So, this time round, you didn't change anything.'

I glanced at Midnight, half expecting him to confirm what I'd said. But instead he took a step back, away from us. His eyes were as dark as his name and he thrust his cane out, pointing it at me.

The air around us erupted like a volcano, and

I grabbed Anna and pulled her close. We were in the eye of the swirling hurricane as Midnight's creatures swept into view. I could barely see them, they were twisting around us so fast. Queuing up to pounce, I thought. A confused mêlée of claws and talons and teeth . . .

Something scaly that might have been a dragon was roaring as it circled. The two grotesque imp-like things had been joined by others and were snapping their sharp teeth together in gleeful anticipation. Other shapes spun and danced round us. Through or between them I could see Midnight laughing.

That's what did it, I think. I wasn't afraid to die, not really. What had I got left? But seeing him laughing – head back and roaring in triumph – that made me angry. Mad. No way was I about to let him win. No way was I about to let him kill me. No way was I about to let him kill Anna.

'Stop!' I screamed. I let go of Anna and flung my arms out wide. I wasn't thinking, wasn't trying, wasn't even *feeling* really. I had no idea how I did it.

But everything did stop. Everything except Midnight. Even Anna. For a moment he continued to laugh. But then he realised that everything else had freeze-framed – the dragon, the imps, gargoyles, grotesques, creatures that make me grow cold and shudder just to remember, things I dared not look at. They were all caught motionless in their deadly dance around us. About to strike. About to feast.

'You're more powerful than I thought,' Midnight said quietly. But the world was silent around us, so I heard him easily. 'You really should join us, you know. Work for me. I can show you how to use these powers. How to control them.'

'No chance. We're going now.' I was surprised at how calm and confident I sounded. 'Don't even think about trying to stop us.'

'Oh, I'll stop you,' Midnight said. He took a step towards us. 'Maybe not today, maybe not tomorrow or even yesterday. But one day I shall stop you. You think you're quite the expert now, don't you? You think you've got powers that can thwart me.'

'Seems I might have,' I said. 'Seems I've got you beaten.'

'Never!' Midnight screamed. It was a sudden explosion of rage and sound as he launched himself towards us, through the ring of frozen creatures, cape flying out behind him and the silver top of his cane jabbing at us.

I grabbed Anna in a hug, reaching round her immobile body to get at my watch. Twist the dial. I didn't really care or know how far or which way I turned it. I just wanted to get away from here and now.

Again the world dissolved round us. Midnight's cry of rage faded. For a moment I thought I saw his creatures leap back into furious life – claws raking and jaws snarling into the middle of the circle. Where we had just been. Where Midnight was now.

Then we were gone.

⏰ 30TH MARCH 1924

It was the interval. There was a crush at the bar as people jostled and fought to buy drinks before the second act.

Anna and I stood getting our bearings. Through the doors to the side of the bar we could see into the theatre. The safety curtain was down. Everyone else seemed very smartly dressed – men in dark suits, women in long dresses. I was surprised to see that Anna was in a long evening dress as well. Her hair was tied in a wide plait and folded back up. She was looking at me a bit oddly, and when I glanced down I saw that I was wearing a dark suit. I could feel the bow tie scraping under my chin.

She looked at her watch – it was about the only thing that hadn't changed, that and her smile. It's a lovely smile.

'1924,' she said. 'Long enough after the events of 1907 to make sure everything is still on track and back to normal.'

'1924 is nearly my bedtime,' I joked.

An old man was pushing his way through the

crowd towards us. His bald head glistened in the glare from the chandeliers. He was carrying three glasses. It was Senex.

'That was very nearly very nasty,' he announced as he handed us each one of the glasses.

I sipped at mine – lemon-flavoured and slightly fizzy.

'You mean the way Midnight nearly ripped time apart,' Anna said.

'Oh, goodness me, no. I mean what those people will do to get a drink.' He raised his glass – he wasn't drinking old-fashioned lemonade, I noticed. Champagne, it looked like. 'Well done, young man. Very good.' He paused to take a sip. 'Yes, very good indeed.' Perhaps he meant the drink.

'Thanks,' I said. 'Seemed to do the trick.'

'And what exactly did you do?' Anna wanted to know. 'It was when I went to find Jane Sinclair, wasn't it? When you went back to the school.'

I nodded. 'It just seemed so obvious. I watched myself, in class. I saw Mike Ibbotson handing out the books. The books with the picture of Jane Sinclair on the cover.'

'The picture I changed.'

'Well,' Senex said quietly, 'yes and no.' He nodded at me to go on.

I shrugged. 'It was easy really. I counted the books he handed out and saw which one I got. Then I swapped the book.'

'You what?'

'I went back to before they were handed out and switched the one I was going to get for a different textbook. Same series, different title.'

She got it now. 'So, different picture on the front.'

'That's right. So after that, when you went back, you went back and changed a different photo. You didn't push Jane out of the way and stand in front of her. It was just some street scene, and you're there in the background. Waving.'

Anna finally understood. She was laughing now. She would have clapped her hands together in glee, except she was holding the glass. 'That's . . . so clever,' she said. 'I remember doing it now, as well. I remember . . .' She hesitated, as if getting her memories in order. 'I just stood there, watching the man with the camera. No girl, no doll. No change to history. And yes, I waved. It was meant to be a postcard from the past, remember. I knew you'd see me on the cover of the book. I was waving to *you*.'

'Not bad,' Senex admitted. He was smiling, though whether in appreciation of what I'd done, or at Anna's changing memory, I don't know. 'Yes, not bad. For a beginner. For a new Runner.'

'He'll get better,' Anna said. 'With the right teacher and some encouragement.'

They were both looking at me like they were thinking about whether to let me join their gang. I suppose they were really.

'Yes,' Senex decided. 'You'll come to understand and to be able to control your powers. You have the makings of an Adept, you know. You'll learn. Over . . .' He paused to give a short laugh. 'Over time.' He took another sip of his drink. 'But now, if you will excuse me, the second act is about to start, and I've only seen this particular performance twice before. And you two,' he added as he turned . . .

I thought he was going to say, 'Well done,' or something like that.

But he didn't.

'You two,' he said, 'have another job to do. In another theatre. Another period of history. Quite an interesting one, in fact.' Then he was off, joining the people streaming back into the auditorium.

'Is that all right?' Anna asked quietly as the people flowed round and past us. As if we weren't really there at all.

'Guess so,' I said. I tried to sound glum and resigned, but I could tell from her expression that my smile gave away what I really thought. 'Seems we're a team, then.'

'Seems we are,' Anna agreed, and she was smiling too. 'So, fancy a trip to the theatre, like the man said?'

'You asking me out?' I asked in mock surprise.

'Sort of,' Anna said seriously. 'What do you say?'

I pretended to consider. 'I'll just finish my drink,' I said, and I smiled at her, raised my eyebrows. 'If we have the time.'

TIME RUNNERS: REWIND ASSASSIN

It's 1596, and Time Runners, Jamie and Anna have been sent on a mission to fix the rips in time and prevent time from falling apart. In sixteenth century London they encounter a man dressed in a modern suit, carrying a sniper rifle, planning an assassination. And the chief candidate seems to be leading playwright William Shakespeare. Sinister Darkling Midnight, surrounded by menacing Skitters, claims to want to form an alliance with the Time Runners, but can he be trusted?

As the Spanish Armada, wrecked and defeated eight years previously, surfaces in the Thames, zombie-like drowned sailors and soldiers leap ashore to invade London. Jamie and Anna will need all their ingenuity and all of Jamie's emerging power over time itself to defeat the Armada yet again and thwart Midnight's dastardly plans.

ISBN: 1416926437 £5.99 pbk
ISBN-13: 9781416926436